Sherlock Holmes

My
Mother's
Diary

By

G. L. Schulze

Sherlock Holmes – My Mother's Diary

This novel is a work of fiction. Names, characters, locations, descriptions, entities, and incidents included in the story are products of the author's imagination. Any resemblance to actual persons, events, and entities is entirely coincidental.

Published by GLS Press

Cover design support by Holli Chlebowski – Graphic Designer

Book photo design by G. L. Schulze

Published in the United States of America

ISBN: 978-0-578-31969-8

Fiction/ General/Action Adventure/Mystery

Other Books by G. L. Schulze

The Young Detectives' Mystery Series:

The Secret Treasure of Pirate's Cove – Book One
The Top Secret Secret of Teddy Rigetta – Book
  Two
The Hidden Secret of Towering Pines Manor –
  Book Three
The Secret of the Sacred Mountain – Book Four
The Secret at the Bottom of Emerson's Cove
  – Book Five
The Secret of the Skeleton Key – Book Six
The Secret of Dead Horse Canyon – Book Seven
The Secret and Murder of Molly Dean – Book Eight
The Secret of PX179 – Book Nine

Sherlock Holmes:

Gray Manor

The Ring and the Box – A Sherlock Holmes Mystery
  Of Ancient Egypt
Sherlock Holmes – The Case of the Dirty Hand – A
  short story published in The MX Book of New
  Sherlock Holmes Stories – Part X: 2018 Annual
Asylum
A Matter of Royal Deception

Sherlock Holmes

My Mother's Diary

Gen Schulze

There are times I find, as one grows older, one's thoughts regress to the past. Memories long forgotten suddenly surface, some most joyous, and others most regrettable.

Such was the case as I sat alone and quite lonely in my old armchair near the window watching the rain spatter against the glass. It ran down in dirty streaks over the sill and collected in muddy puddles on the sodden earth below, so heavy it blurred the light from the gas street lamps outside. It had rained this way for several days now and showed no signs of letting up.

A fire blazed in the grate to ward off the chill and the dampness, but it did nothing to ease the constant ache I always felt in my shoulder on days such as this.

It all began when I was stationed in India, an assistant surgeon in the Fifth Northumberland Fusiliers. My time at Kandahar was short-lived for I was quickly attached to the Berkshires and caught in the thick of the Second Afghan War in the battle of Maiwand. There I had taken a Jezail bullet in my shoulder shattering the bone and sending me on a downward spiral that would take me weeks to recover. I have only my orderly Murray to thank for my life for it was he who managed to escape with me in tow, eventually reaching the British lines and safety.

I think back to those days often, wondering what became of Murray and only realizing now the unforeseen impact such an injury would produce. And I thought often of my old friend Sherlock Holmes. Truth be told, more often than not, lately. I often sat musing about his little black box and the numerous case files tucked away there. Some he allowed me to write and publish accounts of, always telling me I placed too much emphasis on the sensationalism and not enough on the true facts. I took no offense to this for I believe the popularity and the high degree of respect my writings brought him far out-weighed any remonstrations to me. Others he swore me to secrecy, an oath never to reveal for the protection of the parties involved. Always he referred to my writings as a reproach to his incomprehensible study and application of what he would call a logical positivism in the basic theories of criminal investigations.

It is nearly five years since Mr. Holmes and I had a parting of the ways. I to a small boarding house in London, he finally retired to the Sussex coast, purchasing a small villa where he raised and studied bees (of all things). He continued his study on…well…on everything…for that was the way about Mr. Sherlock Holmes.

I must have dozed for I woke with a start. The room was shrouded in shadow, the fire having reduced itself to glowing coals and I saw that the dreary rains had finally ceased and the late afternoon was darkening to evening. I rose stiffly, stretched and decided to avail myself of a short walk before the evening meal and the onset of complete darkness.

The air was still heavy with the smell of the rain, clouds scudded overhead threatening to return but the streaks of deep blue stretched across the western horizon were an indication of a clear sky through the night. With no formal destination in mind, my short walk absentmindedly led me to the old familiar haunts of 221B Baker Street. The years had changed many things. No more were the small family run shops and coffeehouses that once lined Baker Street. These had been purchased by developers and there stood now merchandising shops selling everything from ladies knickers to gentlemen's tobacco.

Gone were the once prevalent telegraph offices. The invention by the American, Bell, called the telephone, now provided instant communications for all.

I stared up wistfully at the old familiar windows at 221B Baker Street and smiled unconsciously when remembering the many hours I spent learning to know and understand this man, Sherlock Holmes, who, to this very day, still remains a mystery. There were times…

…but the laughter of children and their bobbing curly red heads in the windows brought me reluctantly back to the present day. I felt a pang of regret as I turned to go. Regrets over times passage and how unappreciative I had been towards those times in my life that, now as I look back, were the most important.

I turned and retraced my steps to the small apartment I now called home, for I had been faced with having to leave 221B Baker Street upon Holmes's regrettable retirement.

But, it was a fair charge for it; my apartment. A small sitting room and a bedroom. The water closet was down the hall and shared with three other tenants on this floor, but thus far it had presented no problem. An employee of the owner provided cleaning, three meals a day and fresh linens. I counted myself fortunate to have acquired such living quarters. On my diminutive war pension, I was very fortunate indeed.

By the time I reached my apartment it had grown quite dark and I was rather exhausted. I did not realize how far the walk to 221B Baker Street had been and now admonished myself for not taking a cab for the return.

I entered the main hall door and rang for Mrs. Wilson, the housekeeper, for my evening meal. Having just finished my toilet, I saw that she was already at my apartment door with a tray. She, of course, had little company and spoke incessantly when in one's company.

"Just in the nick, Dr. Watson," she was saying. "I am about to take my leave for the evening. Just leave the tray at its usual in the hall. And by the by!" She said. "A call for you, sir, not just moments upon your leaving earlier. The message is on the tray. If that is all, sir, I shall be off."

"Yes, thank you, Mrs. Wilson. Have a pleasant evening," I told her.

"And a good evening to you, sir." She closed the door behind her.

A call? I was taken aback, for rarely these days am I called upon at all. I poured myself a hot steaming cup of tea and reached for the folded sheet of paper on the tray.

Watson, can you come, I need you-
S.H.

It was fortunate that I had set my cup on the tray before reading the note for I surely would be wearing its contents now. Imagine my total unbelieving surprise at the coincidence of this note when it seemed my thoughts had been upon him the entire day. The idea to go or not to go needed no debate. I knew immediately my answer to his summons. I read and reread the note and my excitement grew more at each reading for I would once again be in the company of my dear friend Sherlock Holmes.

I quickly ate a now cold meal and called the train station to check the departure schedule for the first ride to Sussex. I marveled at the wonder of his timely note while I quickly packed a bag and recalled with a somewhat pleasant fondness, that Holmes possessed an uncanny sixth sense ability to read my very thoughts. Had he done that from so far away? I smiled to myself thinking it was a mere coincidence and again recalled that Holmes did not believe in coincidences. Yes…it would certainly be good to be back in his company once more.

The 7:15 to Sussex would mean an early rise and I did not want to miss the train. I decided to retire early and try to get a good night sleep, but the anticipation of seeing my old friend once more kept me wide-eyed most of the night and saw me waiting at the station before 6:30.

I waited on a bench inside the station. A drizzle of chilly rain had begun to fall just before dawn and once again my shoulder told the tale. I thought about his mind reading skills and now grew curious as to the reason for his curt summons. I thought to myself that this was not the reason why I so readily rushed to his side. It was the simple observation in my heart of how dear he had become to me and how much I truly missed his company. I decided I would not allow the constant ache to deter my growing excitement.

When the train finally arrived, I found an empty compartment to the rear and settled near the window once I boarded. I wanted no disturbance and sought only to view the countryside while my thoughts raced and jumbled throughout my head. I need not have feared intrusion, for the passengers were few and my compartment remained empty.

The train ride was swift, rushing me through the dirty London streets and out into the clean fields of the country. Out of a cold drizzling depression and into the bright clear blue sunny skies of anticipation.

I reminisced about my past exploits with Holmes then wondered about the future, about what this summons had in store and before I knew it, the train was already slowing into the Sussex station. It wasn't quite noon yet, so without stopping for an early lunch, I haled a cab and we soon sped down the narrow roadway to Holmes's villa. The driver let me off at the end of the lane which led to Holmes's house. I paid his fare and hoisted my bag to my good shoulder with a renewed energy of old at the excitement I felt about seeing Holmes once more.

It was a short walk up the lane, a most enjoyable walk on a bright sunny day, a mild breeze at my back but as I rounded the last curve and approached the small villa, I was immediately struck with how ill-kept its appearance was. The front of the one story villa was bordered by a white fence that was hardly visible through the masses and tangles of overgrown shrubs and roses that had grown astray. The congestion of flora encircled the entire front yard and threatened to spill over the fence and overtake the lane. The buzzing of what sounded like millions of bees seemed to vibrate the very air about me. And then I understood.

I chastised myself for my earlier thoughts that perhaps Holmes had fallen into ill health and wealth. I had momentarily forgotten. In his retirement he had taken to the raising of bees and was devoting his studies to this cause. Hence, the ample supply of their source for the nectar they required.

Mrs. Garrett, the housekeeper Holmes retained, met me at the door and informed me that Mr. Holmes had gone to the beach some time after breakfast, as was his custom, and had still not returned.

There appeared to be a hint of concern in her voice so, tired as I was from my travels as well as lack of sleep, I deposited my bags inside the door and immediately set out in the direction she indicated.

The small villa of Sherlock Holmes was situated on a beautiful piece of land on the southern slope of the downs. The breeze was brisk here for there were no trees to hold it in check and I held my hat to my brow for fear the wind should blow it back to London.

I approached the edge of the cliffs and stopped to catch my breath. Never in all my born days have I seen a more beautiful vista than that which lay before me. Here rose majestically the huge, chalky white cliffs that ran the coastline and that contrasted sharply with the deep intense blue waters of the Channel. The white, frothy foam of the ocean sprayed a mist into the air with each wild surging wave upon her base giving this vista the appearance of some place magical and mysterious. I could understand immediately why Holmes chose this for his retirement years. It was clearly a place for solitude and thought.

To my right I saw what appeared to be the only means of descending to the beach, a narrow, twisting footpath of dubious character. As there was no other option, I took a deep breath and with much trepidation began my descent carefully picking my way down the narrow, rocky footpath for it was extremely slippery in places and steep enough to caution even the most sure-footed mountain goat.

I stopped on occasion to catch my breath and my balance and took each opportunity to search below for signs of Holmes. But he was nowhere to be seen. Finally nearing the end of the path I still had no sign of him and my heart began to race and I grew fearful of what may await me further along the beach.

Holmes and I had worked through numerous cases together. Some of those adventures nearly cost us our lives, Holmes most particularly. The case which I called 'The Adventure of the Dying Detective', came swiftly to mind now. I recalled Mrs. Hudson, his landlady of 221B Baker Street and how she approached me in extreme panic and fear regarding Holmes who was in a state of serious illness. Upon my return to 221B Baker Street I found him indeed upon his death bed in a most deplorable and wasted state.

He insulted me that day, venomously castigating my professional skills as a doctor. He had insisted...no demanded...that the only person on earth who could save him was a Sumatra planter by the name of Culverton Smith. I went, at Holmes bidding, and I implored the man to come and save my friend's life despite his rebuke of my medical talents. And come he did. But it was soon learned that it was all a ruse and a very cleverly designed one to ensnare the murderer of one Victor Savage and the attempted murder of one Sherlock Holmes.

The weapon, a small black and white ivory trinket box with a sharp spring that pricked the finger upon opening, drawing blood and filling the wound with a deadly poison, causing death following days of intense pain and suffering.

Holmes later apologized for his rebuke upon my medical talents and assured me he held the utmost respect in my astute medical judgments.

The second case I immediately thought of, that which I termed 'The Final Problem' was much more horrible to the mind. It was at this remembering that pain tore through my very being at the loss of Holmes and I prayed this would not be the case once more.

Spring of 1891. I was busy with my practice and my new marriage and had not seen Holmes for some time. Suddenly one evening he came to my home, thin and pale and quite in fear of something. He asked me to accompany him to the Continent and I readily did so. We traveled through Paris and on to Geneva where we came to stay at a little village of the Swiss Alps. On a walking journey through the hills we came upon a long, winding, rocky foot path which led to the falls at Reichenbach. Here, at the bottom of the falls was an immense abyss of incalculable depth which plunged and swelled with the torrential clamor of the melting snows of the Alps.

It was here I was called away on false pretenses. It was here that Sherlock Holmes met his death at the hands of London's most infamous crime boss, Professor

Moriarty. It was here I lost the dearest person in my life and it was here I would live with the guilt in my heart that I had deserted him in his most crucial time of need and it had cost him his life.

I lived with this intolerable guilt, more so through the death of my own very loving wife, Mary. The guilt was mine and only mine to bear and I bore it stoically for more than three years until perchance, one day a wizened book collector appeared in my study. Within seconds his look changed as he threw off his disguise and there before me stood my old and dear friend, Sherlock Holmes, quite alive and well.

He explained to me his motives for that ruse and I vowed to myself that day upon his return, whenever he needed me, I would stand at his side.

Now as I shielded my eyes and scanned the beach I recalled that Holmes was a man of immeasurable brilliance and in some cases reckless daring. He took chances no normal human man would dare to take simply to test a theory or to prove a point. These incidents, I am sure, have begun to take their toll upon him now that he was retired and grown older, for I myself feel the simple aches and pains one seems to acquire with age.

I have not seen him for nearly five years now and I blame myself for not keeping closer contact with the one man who was dearest to me my entire life.

With no sign of Holmes in sight my concern grew. I attempted to rush the last few feet of the path. That was a mistake on my part for the pebbles were loose and slippery and I lost my balance, skidding on the loose pebbles near the end and coming to a teetering stop at the bottom of the treacherous path just barely keeping my footing.

He must have heard the skittering of the stones as well as my exclamation for at the very moment I spotted his thin figure sitting atop a large rock on the beach. When he saw me, he swiftly jumped to his feet and came as quickly towards me as the loose pebbles would allow. I saw he had been reading a letter of some sort but had tucked it into a small black book that disappeared into his pocket.

"My dear Holmes!" I shouted. He hurried forward and embraced me to him in a manner unlike my friend of old.

"Watson! Watson! My dearest and oldest friend! It is so good to see you and so good of you to come so quickly." He had exclaimed with such great exuberance upon his face. "But, I should have known, eh Watson? It is as in the old days. I knew I could count on you once again!"

My fear for his health deepened for never had Holmes displayed any physical, nor stated any verbal emotion such as this.

"Come," he laughed and clapped me on the shoulder. "I shall let you catch your breath then let us slowly and carefully make our way back up this treacherous path that you so nearly took upon the seat of your trousers!"

"Ahhh, you laugh. It is good to bring merriment into an otherwise somber situation," I said "It is wonderful to see you, my old friend. And you should know by now, Holmes, any summons from you I do not question, for I have learned to trust your ways. Now, pray lead the way slowly, for I am still quite winded from its precariously steep descent!"

It was not until we began our formidable ascent up the steep incline that I noticed Holmes in front of me picking his way slowly and stepping with somewhat of a limp. When we reached the top some minutes later, he bent to retrieve a walking stick leaning against a rock nearby. I mentioned my concern to him.

"Old war injury, Watson," he quipped in his usual uncaring characteristic manner. Then he stopped and stared at me with a great intensity and his face grew suddenly very serious. The dark gray blue eyes although faded with age still held that electrifying command that had stopped many a criminal in their footsteps.

"Why, Holmes!" I cried in alarm. "Whatever is the matter?"

He shook his head then and said, "I…it is a long story, my old friend, and one that should not begin here. I am sure Mrs. Garrett has a cold lunch prepared. Let us eat first. My study is as on Baker Street. Comfortable arm chairs, pipes of our favorite tobacco and a roaring fire on the grate. This would surely lend more to the telling of this tale than this rocky ledge. It is there I shall begin." He turned and with the aid of his stick, led the way ahead of me.

I stared at his retreating back for a moment and my thoughts reeled with concern. I could not help the thoughts racing through my head as to what could possibly have occurred that would upset him in such a manner. I dared not express my concern yet because I knew only too well not to press the matter. He would tell me in his own time and in his own way. For that was the way about him. And so I held my concern in check and followed, relieved that I had decided to come. It was good to be in his company once more.

It was well past the lunch hour, however, by the time we cleaned up and settled to eat. A meal had been hastily prepared and for later, left over slabs of cut mutton on fresh bread in the ice chest. Mrs. Garrett did not reside at Holmes's villa, but walked the short distance each day from her tiny cottage at the edge of the little village of Fulworth. Having cleared away the table, she tidied up and soon bid us good day, leaving Holmes and I to our pipes.

We were soon seated comfortably in his study, a warm cozy fire burning on the grate. He had taken all of his effects from 221B Baker Street including the overstuffed sofa and armchairs. It was now on the sofa that I leaned back and lit my pipe, quite content to feel as if this were the old 221B Baker Street once again.

Holmes sat opposite me and I watched with drooping eyelids while he puffed on his pipe, blowing great billowing clouds of gray smoke into the air. His eyes were closed as in days of old, his face usually held no expression. Yet today was different. I did not need his powers of observation to know that the frown upon his face was one of deep turmoil of thought.

Without opening his eyes he said, "You are thinking, Watson, what is so urgent that I have summoned you here and of which I have not spoken of since your arrival."

I was taken aback but for a moment. Then I laughed for I remembered that Holmes always possessed an uncanny ability to read my thoughts.

"That was one thought in my mind, Holmes. But first and foremost, I was simply thinking how wonderful it feels just to be sitting here with you once again."

"Yes. We rather have been remiss with each other," he muttered and fell silent once more. We sat this way for some time content with the peace and tranquility of the moment until the chiming of the mantle clock roused us from our tranquil state.

Holmes then reached into his pocket and withdrew a small leather bound book, the one that I had seen him slip there on the beach earlier. His gazed lingered on its cover for a few moments then he tossed it across to me. It was a small book, old and battered with bent pages and lettering on its cover so faded as to be almost invisible. I turned it to the fire light to read, '*THE DIARY OF JEANNETTE DUBOIS*'. I looked at him with some perplexion and he said,

"There is a note just to the inside of the cover which accompanied the book. You may read it, Watson, then I shall have to give you the facts, at least what I remember of them."

I opened the folded, single sheet of paper and could not possibly imagine how this little black book could be the dilemma of Sherlock Holmes. I read:

Mr. Sherlock Holmes I have recently come to acquire this diary and believe you to know the truth of its contents. I shall call upon you in a fortnight to discuss the matter.

It was simply signed J. M. Dutton.

I sat for some time reading and rereading the single sheet of typewritten words. It had been years since Holmes retired. I knew of nothing in his past that would warrant this almost melancholic defeated behavior in him. "I do not understand, Holmes, what the meaning of this is.

Could this possibly be a client after all these years? Or quite possibly some sort of scandalous trick to blackmail you? Or perhaps someone....does he want money or what?"... my voice trailed off, my mind racing with the possible implications.

Holmes had sat back once again and closed his eyes, and I looked up to see great puffs of smoke nearly obliterating his head and shoulders. There were several long moments of silence before he answered. I waited.

"We cannot determine man or woman, Watson, for obviously this person has gone to great lengths to hide their identity. The note is typewritten, posted from London. No fingerprints on the note itself or the envelope as I have already tested it. Could be a woman wearing gloves, could be a man being very careful and doing the same...but speculation is in itself a measure of doubt.

"The diary itself is old but," he sighed heavily, sadness and despair etched upon his features. "Ahhh...Watson, Watson. There is something, my old friend, that I am going to tell you that I have told no other person...not even Mycroft...not the whole of it, anyway... perhaps I should have...but...well...there is no steering clear of it now."

I saw that he completely avoided answering my concerns so I did not press that issue. Apparently there were more important matters that he needed to speak of. "Holmes, my good man, you are speaking in a blabber of incoherent mumbling. Have you read the diary?"

"No...no...but I am certain I already know its contents, Watson. Pour us a drink and I shall begin."

"I must take you back to the spring of 1891. Remember? You accompanied me on a week's journey to the Continent and it was here you thought I had truly met my demise."

"Yes, of course. How could I not remember? The thoughts of that journey crossed my mind only today, Holmes. The shock, the pain…it was a cleverly executed plan, but what…"

Holmes waved a hand through the thick smoke with his customary air of impatience and I closed my gaping mouth, ready to listen.

"If you recall how I related to you my hiding place on the rock ledge above the falls and my immediate and perilous descent down to avoid the rocks being pelted upon me from one of Professor Moriarty's cronies. I also told you I had escaped and went into hiding throughout Europe and America until such time that I felt it was safe to return. But…my dear friend…" and at this he leaned forward towards me and continued in a hushed tone, "but…I did not tell the complete truth."

I made to protest but he cut me short again.

"Please forgive me that liberty. It was to some degree because of your reaction upon my return that I feared, should I tell the whole of my adventurous death, it might perhaps precipitate a heart's malfunction upon your part to learn the truth. Your fainting upon my sudden return, after all, led me to realize the full extent of your complete admiration and caring for me, and I did not wish to displace that."

I stared at Holmes now with a look of complete and utter disbelief. Why…the presumptuousness of the man! How could he…how dare he…yes once again he had read my feelings through my reactions so completely! Feelings that I had not dared to admit to myself until only recently how much I had come to care for and admire him. He was continuing on as though it were the most natural conversation, one we'd had numerous times and so I came back to listen once more.

"I am truly sorry," he continued seemingly oblivious of my distress, "for not confiding in you then, but…but…it was a part of my personal life that I did not wish to discuss with anyone. And now, my good Watson, in retrospect, I believe it was a part of my life I did not know *how* to discuss with anyone."

I sat motionless on the sofa, staring dumfounded at him and now I had no words to utter. He closed his eyes once more and with a heavy sigh, leaned wearily back in his chair. Somehow, as I looked at him, he appeared sad and shrunken, having lived through some horrible ordeal he felt was too disturbing for another human to share.

"But Holmes," I finally managed. "Surely our friendship was worth more than your suppression of whatever horrendous ordeal had befallen you?"

He opened his gray-blue eyes slowly. Eyes that would normally be commanding and determined but were now apologetic and filled with remorse and he looked into mine. "After all these years, Watson, I believe I have convinced myself that I did not tell you because I did not wish to diminish myself in your eyes."

I was so stunned that all that came from my mouth was a mumbled stutter until I simply stared at him and sat quiet.

"You see," he sighed heavily once more. "It is as I feared. My one true friend in my entire life and now it appears I have alienated him, also."

At this I finally managed to find my tongue and said to him, "My old friend Sherlock Holmes. It gives me the utmost pleasure to inform you that with all your keen powers of deductions and reasonings, oh, and include mind reading, you have read me wrong for the first time in our entire relationship.

"In all my travels and with all those I have met and associated with, it has been my utmost pleasure and honor to call you friend. You hold a place so very dear in my heart, Holmes, that I feel you are as a brother to me. There is not one thing in this entire world that you could possibly have said or done that would ever diminish yourself to me."

He looked at me and I believe at that very moment, it was the first time in my acquaintance of Sherlock Holmes that I thought I saw the brightness of tears upon his face.

"Good old Watson. You honor me far more as one man than all those faithful readers who so followed your romanticized accounts of my cases." He smiled now, a smile that spread across his face and affected all his features and it seemed the strained, exhausted look one carries of hidden guilts and secrets slipped away from him. He leaned back into the chair to puff his pipe and said wearily, "I am tired today, Watson."

"As am I," I responded. The uneasiness between us had passed and once more one could feel the old comfortableness and bond that had always existed between me and the great Sherlock Holmes.

He rose then, apologizing once more. "Forgive me. I had quite forgotten you had only just arrived today. Let us retire and start afresh in the morning."

Within the hour I lay in my warm comfortable bed and felt more content than I had in years. My last thoughts were of my resolve to do whatever possible to help my old friend through this situation whatever that may be.

I woke to a bright sun shining in my eyes and the constant twittering and whistling of bluebirds and wrens outside my window. Stretching before the large French doors that opened onto a terrace at the back of the lawn, I saw Holmes bent forward over his beehives just a hundred feet down. He worked carefully and slowly for he wore no netting for protection. I recalled something he had said to me once a long time ago, said in passing really, although the circumstances were different. He said to establish a trust….that is the key.

I watched and marveled at how calmly he stood amongst them. Hundreds, perhaps thousands of bees buzzing around him from head to foot and I saw how delicately he walked amongst them with no harm, to either party. I smiled to myself and I recalled that that was the way about Sherlock Holmes. Calm and confident in the face of danger. . .regardless the danger.

Except for the diary.

His confidence seemed to grow more scant by the hour and the calmness seemed to seep out of him at each mention of the thing as if there was something in his past that haunted him. Haunted his very soul. I shuddered at the thought.

He had finished for he now ambled through the rows of hives towards the house and I saw a hand as he caught me in the window. I waved back and dressed quickly, meeting him a few minutes later for breakfast. I put my fears and concerns to the back of my brain to try to sort them out later, perhaps once the diary shed fresh light on past events. I did not wish Holmes to read my thoughts on these matters.

"My most favorite place, second to the laboratory," he indicated his bees and reached to butter his toast. "Let us eat. Then we'll go to the beach. It is quiet there and we will bring along the diary. I do believe it is time we begin to learn the truth."

He appeared to be in much higher spirits than the day before and I saw that his limp was not as noticeable. But then, it was a warm, sunny morning and the constant ache of my shoulder had also lessened.

We strolled lazily down the walk then carefully chose our footing down the steep treacherous path. I marveled that Holmes traversed this path for his existence here and never saw to constructing a means of easier descent. I wanted to mention this to him, but keeping my balance as he sure-footedly stepped ahead of me became my main concern. Once we reached the bottom, he allowed me to catch my breath then led me along the beach over the loose pebbles and stones some fifty yards ahead.

Here I saw a beautiful little hollow where the water lapped lazily against the giant rock outcrop of the great white cliffs towering above us. The noise of the surf against the rocks was muted here and I understood why Holmes chose this beautiful spot for his concentrations. We soon found comfortable seating, he sitting on a large rock, I on a patch of warm, dry sand with a large rock as a back rest.

"Remember back to 1891, Watson, for it was there it all began. In May I believe. We traveled to Switzerland, to the village of Meringen. Remember? Near the falls of Reichenbach?" he asked.

"How could I ever forget. It was where…well, where I thought you had died, Holmes!" I shuddered once more at the thought.

"Yes. I am indeed sorry for that, old chap. I did explain later that I had managed to escape across the Alps and found myself in Florence. But here, my friend, I am afraid is where the story is not true. Not entirely."

I waited patiently because I knew he really didn't want an answer from me. His gaze swept across the water and lingered for a moment before he continued.

"Yes, I did scramble down that rocky cliff and I did escape through the mountains. But in my haste to avoid the assault of thrown rocks from above, I lost my footing part way down and was sent tumbling to the bottom. I hit the trail hard but immediately picked myself up and ran, but did not have full knowledge of my injuries."

"Injuries! Good lord Holmes, you…" once again he held up that impatient hand of his to silence me and the look on his face was enough to do just that. It seemed once he started, he had a need to keep going. I shut up to listen.

"I do remember that I traveled through the night across the mountains finally falling into an exhausted sleep near dawn. When I woke hours later I was not only cold and hungry, but very weak from loss of blood. My legs had collapsed beneath me in the night and when I attempted to move I was met with the most excruciating pain. It appeared that on my altogether too swift descent from the cliffs, I fell the last few feet into a dead and very dried tree, one jagged branch of which was now protruding from my thigh."

"My lord, Holmes! The pain must have been unbearable!" I cried for I could hold still no longer.

"Indeed so, Watson, indeed so. But I had no means with which to correct the matter nor the strength to remove it myself and so found myself a sturdy branch for a walking stick and managed to get up and continue on. Mind you, I don't remember much at all after that other than I kept falling and getting up over and over. I had to keep moving to prevent myself from freezing to death. Although, it did occur to me much later that my actions surely should have caused me to die from loss of blood rather than from the cold.

"I do not recall passing out of Switzerland, but I apparently did so. The next coherent recollection I have is when I opened my eyes once more, I found myself in a small cottage on a bed near a warm fire somewhere in the south of France."

"Good lord, Ho…" I began and suddenly realized I was beginning to sound like a skipping phonograph. "What a business Moriarty turned out to be!"

"Indeed…" He reached inside his pocket and now withdrew the small black book. He stared at the cover and I could see his eyes linger on its title, '*THE DIARY OF JEANNETE DUBOIS*'. His eyes slowly shifted from the cover to me, and with a heavy sigh he handed it to me and said, "Here. Inside this little black book of memories I am sure will explain all that I cannot. Would you please begin to read, Watson?"

His voice had softened and he spoke in a hushed tone and I saw that despite the anguish of having his past secrets revealed, there was also an air of excitement at the prospect of finally learning the book's contents. I also saw there was a shadow of apprehension and I grew to believe that something happened to Holmes that was so absolutely horrendous that even he had erased it clean from his memory. I conjured horrible scenes in my mind and…

"Watson!" he woke me from my daydream of nightmares. "Would you read, please?"

We settled ourselves more comfortably on the white sand inside the tiny hollow and I took the small book in hand. It was written in French so I do hope that the reading public will forgive me the indulgence of its translation into English which I have put to pen below. The first page read in quite plain letters,

----

"THE DIARY OF JEANNETTE DUBOIS"

I, Jeannette Dubois, have never had the need to put my life onto paper, but the events of these last few days have become too complex and...yes...even intriguing, that I feel it is now necessary to do so. If only for myself, to remind me that this was no dream. I shall go back one week to begin at the beginning. I know how the memory fails as one ages so I will write here all that happens.

For my children.

May 8, 1891

I am a widow living alone. My husband, Josef, was killed in the mines. I have a tiny, one room cottage outside of a small village and I sell goods at the village market for my living. I have hens for fresh eggs and a small herd of goats for their rich milk and cheese. I do not make much, but my needs are few. I save what I can to go to America. That is my dream.

Today, I was up early as I always am to collect the fresh eggs and prepare the cured cheese for the market. There was a white layer of crispy frost on the ground and it crunched beneath my feet. The sun was just rising through the heavy branches of the tall pines of the forest and my hen house was still dark from its shade.

I lit the lantern just inside the door and was so frightened at the sight I nearly dropped it from my hand. I could not move for fear for there was a man lying on the floor. He looked dead and I did not know what to do. I wanted to turn and run for the police, but my feet would not lift me from the spot. But soon, the cold air from the open door woke me to my senses and I knew I could not leave this dead man here.

With no one to help me, I had no choice but to drag him to the outside and then I decided I should summon the police. I reached for his legs to pull, but had barely moved him when he groaned and rolled to his side.

I screamed and drew back against the wall, frightening my hens. Their clattering made me realize he must get out of there. I did not know how I would do this, for he was so severely injured and cold as the morning frost.

My heart was racing with fright. I knew I had to do something. I decided I would drag him to the forest, away from me, to die, for surely he would. He was no matter to me. Probably running from the law and I wanted no part of this. I bent to see his face and his eyes flew open so suddenly I fell stumbling to the floor beside him! He grabbed my arm and held with such fierceness and tried to speak. But all I could understand was "wat...mor...safe."

He cried this over and over and as frightened as I was I tried to calm him and get him to let me loose. But it was of no use. He was still very strong despite his injuries. Still holding on to me he struggled to his feet. I could not believe there was any strength left in him for he was thin and pale and wore more blood on his clothing than was left inside his body. He would not let go and so together we staggered across the slippery path to the house. I could not leave him to die. Not now.

He was out of his head with fever and once inside I could hold him no longer and he crumpled in a heap to the floor near the fire.

I stared at him now for my fear was beginning to lessen and I knew I should go to the police, but I did not. Instead, I put water on the fire to boil and stripped him of his clothing and shoes. I bathed him as best as I could then wrapped him in blankets warmed by the fire.

He lay still unconscious and I prayed he would not awaken for I left the most horrible task until last. His left hip was swollen black and purple and the green of infection oozed from the tear in the flesh where a large object was pierced inside. He had lost so much blood, his clothes were soaked and ragged.

I took a deep breath and did it quickly. I pulled with great difficulty at the object until finally it wrenched free, tearing the flesh. I grew sick at the sight. I saw then it was a tree branch, old and twisted and dripping with blood so I threw it into the fire. Blood poured from the gaping torn wound and I feared that now he surely would die. I worked as quickly as I could to clean the wound but it was torn open and jagged and I knew it must be stitched before the wrap could be put to it.

I was exhausted by the time all was done. I thank the Lord he remained unconscious because I would not have known what to do should he have awakened. He groaned now and then but did not awaken. I finally finished and sat back against the warm stones of the fireplace to catch my breath and regain my senses. I found myself shaking, not only from my exertions, but from the frightening thoughts of now what to do with this fugitive. It was getting late. The morning was already giving way to noon.

I sat for some time staring at this man who was so very tall, so thin and pale. His hands and face were covered with scratches and small cuts from fighting and stumbling through the heavy brush of the mountain forests. The white color of his face was only changed by the blue tinge around his lips and eyes where his skin had darkened by the freezing frosts of the cold mountain nights. Surely a fugitive running from the police for no sane man would run to be lost in the forests in such a condition. I thought once more of the police but instead searched through his bloody clothes. There was no identification papers. Only some English shillings and a small notebook and pencil. I put these in a small envelope and put it in my wooden trunk under a window near the door. His clothes I tossed into the fire. They were beyond repair.

He was resting now so I finished my chores. I did not wish to leave him, but leave I must. I had to bring my items to the market. Each franc I saved would bring me closer to America. I looked one last time at him near the fire before I left. He had not moved. I prayed he would not awaken and try to run away. I went to the market.

I glanced up at Holmes sitting across from me on the beach. His eyes were closed, his face expressionless, but I knew he was drawing every word to him. Fascinated with the words of the diary, I continued to read.

May 9, 1891

He sleeps badly, this fugitive. The fever has worsened through the night and I could not understand how he managed to survive up to now through the cold, freezing nights of the mountains. For me, it was a long, sleepless vigil. He woke once and stood up so quickly I could not stop him. He stared about him like a crazy man looking to escape, seemingly oblivious of the pain in his leg and the blood seeping through the bandaging. He did not stop me when I cautiously drew my single bed to the fire towards him. It was some time, before he began to fall forward, and he allowed me to touch him and make him comfortable on the bed. He cried for water, but I dared not for fear the retching would cause harm far worse than was already upon his starved body.

I mixed a tea of peppermint and honey with a touch of ginger root to settle the craving in his stomach. He drank greedily. The wound had bled fresh so once again I cleaned it and put a fresh dressing. This time I applied a healing salve before the dressing.

It strikes me once more how tall he is for he reaches head to toe upon my small bed. His face is so very thin and his nose is large, perhaps broken at some time and it sits on his face as a hawk's His brows were thick, seeming to meet in the center and his dark hair was unkept and tangled to his collar. The beard stubble on his face told me he had been this way for some days. There was something about this fugitive that interested me. I cannot say what.

He is finally sleeping once more. Sometimes moaning with the fever, sometimes calling out 'WATSON!' I am eager to learn about this Watson.

"Good lord, Holmes!" I exclaimed and I set the black book aside. "This is most extraordinary! Did you know? Did you remember any of this?"

"I had no idea of what transpired, Watson, for we never spoke of that time at all. Things were so strange in the beginning and after...well...after there were so many...so...well...other matters, you might say," Holmes said. He rose stiffly from the sandy beach and checked his timepiece. I knew instantly this was his way of telling me he did not wish to speak of the matter.

"We have been here quite some time, it seems. I do believe Mrs. Garrett should have our lunch on the table. Come, Watson. We shall eat and perhaps continue this intriguing disclosure in the gardens."

"Very good, Holmes. I am rather hungry and a fresh hot cup of tea would do nicely about now." I handed him the small book and he replaced it carefully, lovingly inside his pocket. I knew better than to question him now regarding anything in the diary thus far. Besides, he himself stated he had no knowledge of what had transpired. Yet, the events of the small book had us both lost in our own thoughts as we walked across the beach towards the path.

There was silence still as we made our way carefully up the path. My mind raced over and over the words in the diary. Poor Holmes! I had been feeling piteously sorry for myself at the loss of my friend and all the time he had been fighting for his very existence! I chastised myself for my shortcomings. We were close friends and had shared many adventures together. I felt because of this bond that perhaps I should have felt *something* was remiss at the time, but my own self-pity prevented me from feeling anything else.

We finally reached the top and at the landing Holmes turned to me, a look of mild reproach upon his weathered face. He said, "Good old Watson. Do not persecute yourself over this matter. You had no means of knowing I was still alive somewhere, for all the clues I left behind were too convincing to believe otherwise."

"Damn it, Holmes!" I shouted at him. "How on earth *DO* you do that?"

He laughed, a loud and hearty laugh and I shook my head in wonder at his uncanny ability to know my very thoughts. I was immediately pleased to see something of my old friend Holmes returning.

"It is the simplest of deductions," he said and we laughed together on our way to the house, the disturbing words of the diary put behind us; for the moment at least.

Sherlock Holmes was never a man who chatted easily about his personal life. Why…when I first became acquainted with him, it was some years before I came to know he even had an older brother, Mycroft, who held some special secretive title of important anonymity with His Majesty's Secret Service, I believe, and was hardly ever mentioned. There was never a need to talk much about our past lives, our families. We were always too busy solving cases and simply getting on with our day to day lives in London.

And so the years had passed. Too many by my recollections, for here we were, now two elderly men, now sharing aspects of our lives that brought us closer than we ever were.

Lunch was a delicious and easy affair as was always with Mrs. Garrett, and soon we were strolling down the stone path of his backyard into his overgrown and flower crowded garden beds, all of which provided ample nectar for his bees. The diary had not been mentioned since the beach and I left it that way. I saw his gaze wander and without a word he headed towards the hives, leaving me behind with my own thoughts.

He alone walked in amongst them, unprotected, to take in another inspection. Here I saw him pull out his little notebook of which he was never without, and as he walked here and there, he jotted down some new development or change in the constant and continuous habits of his precious bees.

I casually leaned against the gate post content to just watch when once again I was struck with the feeling of how wonderful it was to be, once more, in the company of my dearest friend.

My thoughts wandered back to the entries in the diary and I shuddered at the picture conjured up in my mind's eye. Holmes freezing, stumbling, starving and bleeding to death through the unforgiving Swiss alpine mountains and forests and how completely unaware I was of this entire torturous period of his life.

I shuddered even more when I recall that eventful day three years later when an elderly book collector appeared in my study and in the blink of an eye stood before me as

Sherlock Holmes. The shock of seeing him still alive and standing in front of me, sent me reeling to the floor in a faint, the one and only time in my life. I remembered later how thin and exhausted he looked and now I wince with the horror of what he must have been subjected to while traveling through those lost three years of feigned death.

I shook my head and returned to the present. He was carefully leaving the buzzing hives and was speaking to me as he approached…

"…for my next treatise on bees…why Watson…I do believe you were not paying any attention whatsoever!" He exclaimed to me.

"I am so very sorry, Holmes old chap, but your keen deductive senses are correct as usual. I admit I was day dreaming and your conversation completely escaped me."

"Ah! It is of little consequence," he replied. "Come. Let us relax the rest of the day away." He led the way through a small, whitewashed arbor half obscured by the vines of trailing red roses, and into a neat patio area where we settled nicely on a couple of rattan chairs. The day was still quite warm and it appeared that Mrs. Garrett possessed the sixth sense of my friend for at the precise moment we sat, she appeared with a tray of iced tea, small finger sandwiches and tiny raspberry jelly scones.

"I shall take leave the remainder of the day, Mr. Holmes, if you please. I have church business to attend in the village. A cold supper is put up in the ice chest, sir."

"Very well, Mrs. Garrett, and thank you," Holmes replied.

We sipped at the cold refreshing mint tea to which she had added a tangy slice of lemon and nibbled at the sandwiches and scones. Lunch it seemed had only been a short time ago, but it appeared that the fresh country air provided one with an excuse to eat whatever is put before him at any given time of the day. It wasn't long before we settled down to a good pipe. Blue gray swirls of smoke curled and rose, then drifted on the light breeze to the east. It was then that Holmes withdrew the diary from his pocket once more. I noticed that once again his eyes lingered on its title for a moment longer than necessary before he handed me the small, worn book. "If you would be so kind, Watson."

I took the book in hand as I set my pipe down. Holmes leaned his head against the back of his chair and closed his eyes, ready to listen.

I opened the book to its mark and began to read.

May 12, 1891

The day has come, a gray dawn. Clouds poured down a heavy, icy rain all day leaving the paths and roadways too dangerous to travel. I did not go to the village today but remained at my cottage. I took care of my hens and goats then returned to the comfort of the fireplace. My fugitive rested, fitful at times, for the fever was still heavy upon him.

It has now been four days since I first found him. His fever is still at a high pitch and he tosses and moans with the pain. The wound is still very swollen and red. I clean and change the dressing three, sometimes four times each day, but only when he is not fitful because it is at those times he pushes me away. Today I see a good sign. The black marks of poison are no longer there and I no longer fear he will lose his leg.

But the fever. The fever rages inside of him and I do not know what else to do. I have heard told that a high fever for a long time affects the brain and one is no longer right in the head. I pray this is not so.

It must have been fate that caused me to save some of Josef's clothing. I have taken them from my trunk and set to altering them on this chilly day. Josef was broad in the chest and the shirts will not be a problem. This man is so thin and wasted from the starvation, he will fit. The trousers I must let down several inches at the cuffs and I feared they would still be not long enough. But he will have some warm clothes to wear.

He cries and mumbles in his fever always of this 'Watson' and 'Safety'. I find myself wishing he was well so I may learn more of this Watson.

May 13, 1891

What a terrible night this has been! It was late and I had just fallen to sleep when suddenly I was awakened by the frantic screaming and shouting of my fugitive. I feared the fever had truly destroyed his mind.

He was sitting upright on the bed staring madly about him and into the air, shouting 'WATSON! WATSON! MORIARTE!' I was too afraid to approach him that he may try to do me harm.

He dragged his legs over the side of the bed to stand and it was at this very moment our eyes met. Mine filled with fear where I crouched backed into the corner near the end of the fireplace, his deranged and wild with maddening fever where he sat on the edge of the bed. I could see the fever hot and raging on his face, the whites of his eyes bulging from the red, swollen sockets.

Sweat stood upon his brow and he swiped at it with the back of his hand. I jumped at the movement. He was breathing so very heavy I felt his chest would burst. I clutched my blanket to me and stayed as a statue.

He stared at me until I thought my own heart would stop and tremble me to the floor. Then suddenly, out of nowhere, through the maddening silence, he said, "It is as you say, Watson. He is dead." Then he fell back upon the bed sideways.

I waited for a long time too afraid to approach him. When I realized I myself was shivering from the cold, I came to my senses. He lay unconscious on the bed and had not moved for some time. I got up and carefully returned him to the bed and wrapped the blankets about him. I made fresh the fire.

I was no longer afraid now so I sat on the edge of the bed looking at him. The fever, it seemed, had broke and I saw that the red flush of his face began to fade and his breathing came much easier. It was a moment before I chanced to see that his hand had fallen to his side and now rested upon mine.

"Holmes! This is utterly horrible! In all my days at hospital after my war injury I do not believe I witnessed such an account as this!" I cried.

"I, too, am taken aback, Watson. A whole week of my life had vanished without my knowledge. Fever is a damaging mystery, is it not? And, one, I am afraid, even my shrewd methods and keen powers of deductions cannot explain," Holmes said.

"But this woman! To have taken you in and not inform the police...she obviously thought you a criminal... or...perhaps she herself was deranged?" I queried.

"No, Watson. Not in the least. I do recall, which was the last bit of memory at the moment, one cold, star filled night as I lay huddled starving and freezing beneath the branches of a thick pine, that I was severely injured and would probably die. The next coherent image is one of opening my eyes one morning and realizing I had not.

"I remember lying quite still because the strangeness of my surroundings took me quite by surprise. It certainly wasn't the pine tree branches of my last recollections. I was weak and filled with pain and hunger but I managed to inch up to lean upon my elbow and...there she was. This woman. Lying on the floor sleeping near the dying fire."

"The floor, Holmes?"

"Why yes. It is quite obvious, is it not, Watson? Reading from the diary the woman was of ill means, attested to by her one room cottage and single small bed to which she refers to. And if I were on that bed, she had no other recourse but the floor," he quickly responded with some exasperation.

He continued more calmly, ignoring my muttered attempt to explain myself. "She was not an overly beautiful woman, Watson, but as I watched her sleep, I came to see she was quite handsome. Her hair was dark, almost black and by the dying embers of the fire glistened with touches of red. Her eyebrows were perfect, one to the other rising in tiny arches in the center. Her nose was pert and her mouth set full betneath high cheekbones. No...she was not a beauty, Watson, but she was pleasing to the eye, nonetheless. And when suddenly her eyes opened to stare back upon me, I saw they were a startling blue, near cobalt, and bright and beautiful."

I stared at this old friend of mine for a moment, picturing this woman in my mind. I said, "Why Holmes, I did not realize there was a touch of a romantic buried beneath that ever persistent deductive exterior."

"I have never considered myself as possessing any of the sort of romantic notions that the ordinary male possesses, Watson. However, it did not take too long, even in my distressed condition, for me to understand that this woman had saved me from death and I certainly looked upon her with a keen sense of appreciation that I have never thought of towards another female."

"But...surely Holmes...you must have..." I began, but he waved an impatient hand to me, as was his way sometimes and interrupted me.

"Would you continue reading, please." And he leaned back in his chair, closing his eyes clearly dismissing any further conversation.

I understood him only too well for this was his customary play whenever a subject was approached of which he clearly did not wish to speak. I was dismayed for there were many questions I wanted to ask, too many answers I needed to clear up the mass of thoughts racing through my mind. I knew to question him would avail me nothing. So, I continued with the diary.

It is now the dawn and I opened my eyes only to be stared upon by my fugitive. His eyes were a handsome dark, gray-blue and no longer held the distant glassy look of the fever. I rose slowly to not frighten him but mostly because I was a little frightened for myself. I did not know what would happen now that he was out of his fever. I wrapped my blanket about me.

"Good morning, Monsieur," I said to him with a forced smile. "I see you have decided to rejoin the living after all."

But he only stared for a while longer then closed his eyes and lay back on the bed and I thought to myself it is because he does not speak or understand French.

I had tied a sheet across the walls in one corner of the room and I went there now to quickly change. I built up the fire in the stove and put a kettle to boil. I knew now that with his fever gone he would need food to regain his strength and to heal properly.

He was so very weak, he tried bravely to feed himself, but more was down the front of his bed clothes than he managed into his mouth. He finally agreed to allow me to help. He seems a very proud man, my fugitive.

After he finished eating, I cleaned up and then it was time to change the dressings before I went about my chores. His voice rose angrily to me that I should not touch him, he would manage.

I left him, hurt and angry that he should speak to me so. I gathered my eggs quickly, destroying some in my haste and anger. It was already late and I hastened into my cool cellar beneath the earth to gather the cheeses stored there that were ready for the market. I would go today. My hens were exceptional layers this past night and I had more than my usual baskets ready to go.

I tied my large goat to the small two wheeled cart and set off. It was just as well because I would need extra provisions to help my fugitive regain his strength. I was still so very angry at his manner that I did not even stop in to see how he was managing. But I did not care. Let him manage.

I had gotten a late start and so it was late and beginning to get cold when I finally returned and put away the cart, leaving the goat to graze. I entered my cottage with an arm load of wood for the fire just as the sun was beginning to set behind the trees. He was sitting up leaning against the back of the bed, looking very pale and exhausted.

He said to me in a very weak voice as I bent to replenish the dying embers of the fire, "I do apologize, Madam, for my rudeness earlier. It appears that you are correct and I am compelled to be a burden to you. I did not fully understand the severity of my injuries nor the complete debilitation of my strength. If you would assist…and…please accept my sincere apology."

This time, he spoke in French to me, his voice was barely above a whisper but I could tell he had a beautiful English speech and a gentle tone, this proud man. I immediately put aside my anger from the morning.

"There is no need for apology, Monsieur. I have always been correct with you, and only wish to help you to be yourself again. That is all."

I built the fire in the stove and put water to boil. I peeled potatoes and vegetables into a pot of boiling water for soup and quickly made up dough for fresh biscuits. Already the chill inside the cottage was warming to the glow of the fire in the grate. He allowed me then to change the dressing. The wound now held no sign of infection and the swelling and redness were also quickly leaving.

"You have had a doctor here to stitch the wound then?" he asked when he saw the stitches.

"No, Monsieur. I stitched the wound myself. It may be painful, but I will have to remove them in a few days. See, it is healing now quite nicely."

"So you are an entrepreneur of many talents," he smiled weakly up at me.

"Oui, Monsieur. My husband, Josef was killed in the mines two years ago and I have had to learn many things to survive." I told him as I worked. "I am saving my money to go to America. I hear there is opportunity for anyone to take. I want to make a new start there, Monsieur."

He lay back on the bed suddenly looking more pale and tired than before. "America. Yes America is a good place to go. Perhaps we will both go to America, Madam."

I could not help it but my heart jumped in my breast. While I watched him sleeping later, I reasoned to myself that he did not ask me to go WITH him. He merely said he would like to go.

And yet...

I slowly closed the diary and looked up at Holmes sitting across from me. I was surprised at the calmness of his features given the words I'd just read out of the diary for I, myself was stunned beyond words. His eyes were closed and it gave every appearance that he was sleeping.

"No. I do not believe I asked her to go to America, Watson. I was merely thinking, at the time, that perhaps America would make an excellent opportunity for two reasons. One, allow me time to investigate further into that country and its society, if only to satisfy my own curiosity. Two, it would be the perfect place for me to go into hiding until such time it would be safe, from the Moriarty gang, for me to return."

"Well," said I finally finding my tongue, "it was certainly being construed that way, Holmes."

"Yes, I see that it was. But she never brought it up again and nor did I. Not until much later, when I was more able to travel. But look!" He exclaimed getting to his feet rather quickly. I knew this was another of his ploys to dismiss any continuation of this conversation. "We have been so engrossed in this diary we have hardly noticed how low the sun has set. Fetch up the tray would you, Watson old chap. We shall forage through the ice chest for our cold supper."

I did as he bade me because I knew any protestations on my part would be unheeded. There was plenty of time to return to the diary. Plenty of time to ask the questions I had and push for the answers that I hoped would answer everything.

Mrs. Garrett was certainly very knowledgeable in the ways of Sherlock Holmes. Inside the ice chest were thick cut slabs of roasted meats and cheeses and breads. All that was required of us was to put them together. A full kettle of water, still warm atop the stove, only needed to be reheated and soon we carried trays of fat mutton and beef sandwiches and a large pot of fresh brewed tea into the study.

We talked of trivial news and events near the fire as we ate. Once again my mind drifted back to those numerous evenings when Holmes and I would sit near the fire and discuss affairs of the day amidst the muted background of the hustle and bustle of London outside our window.

But this was different. There was no clacking of horse carriages over the cobbled stoned streets, no chattering of passersby on the pavements below. Instead was the quiet solitude of the country evening that slipped quietly into darkness outside where it seemed, even the birds and bees settled into silence, and the crackling of the wood on the fire our only background disturbance.

Once the trays were set to the side, I saw him pat his breast pocket for his pipe and I rose to fetch the old familiar shoe of Raggs tobacco on the mantle.

"Ah, Watson, I see you are beginning to read *my* mind," he laughed. "I have always felt that a good pipe after a meal is a wonderful and relaxing treat to the end of a day, is it not?"

"Absolutely!" I replied. The sandwiches were rich and

quite sumptuous and the tea brewed just strong enough to warm away the chill and send a feeling of tranquility through the soul. I was as content as content could be, not only to have enjoyed such a treat, but to be able to be sitting here with Holmes once again. We filled our pipes and sat together puffing great clouds of smoke for some time in a mutually contented silence. I broke the silence finally saying, "Tell me, my dear Holmes. This diary. Do you believe it to be genuine?"

"Of course the diary is genuine, Watson. I can vouch for that for it carries too much truth to be anything but. It is, however, the owner of the diary I question."

"How so?"

"Look here," he suddenly leaned forward. "It has been close to twenty years since these events have occurred. Anyone could have gotten hold of this book (he tapped the diary on the table) and decided to…well…as you implied earlier on the day of your arrival…blackmail me."

"Blackmail!" I shouted. "Why…whatever for?" Then I remembered back at my first reading of the letter that these were my exact thoughts even though I muttered them more to myself than aloud, surprised yet relieved that he had heard.

"Come, come Watson!" he cried. "Think about this. Obviously here in the pages of this little black book are the makings of an intriguing love affair. All the subtle hints are already in place. A love affair of the world's greatest detective, Sherlock Holmes! A man who has not once ever glanced at a woman and now…now shows himself to be nothing but a mere mortal man with the same longings and lust for women as any other man. Think what that would do to my reputation, Watson. I am of a mind to believe this J. M. Dutton is as our old friend Charles Milverton. Remember? He who blackmailed for the money out of sheer spite!"

"Surely, Holmes, if there were a love affair…if in your heart…I mean…if the words in the diary are true, and I say if, then should that be so difficult to bare? And, at that, what would there leave to blackmail?" I asked.

He sat for some time leaning forward, staring intensely at me. I watched as the hard lines on his face changed from anger and consternation, then softened into a peaceful look of mild acquiescence. "No, Watson, it would not." He sighed heavily and leaned back into the chair. "I am an old man now, and although I have always prided myself to be impeccably gallant where a woman's concerns are, I am not ashamed of the words in this diary. I am only ashamed that it has taken me all my life to admit them, and how this person may misconstrue its contents."

I have had the acquaintance of the man sitting before me for most of my life and yet to this day *still* do not know the man at all. My heart swelled as I now looked through different eyes at my old friend Sherlock Holmes. The love and respect I now felt for him was immeasurable. I saw now that his relationship with that woman, whatever that relationship was, was as personal to him and him alone as the deep and trusted friendship and caring he held for me. I also saw the turmoil of self-persecution he battled within himself over this entire situation and how difficult it was for him to come to terms with it.

I recalled the words of the diary, of Holmes calling out to me 'WATSON!' in his delirious fever to warn me of Moriarty and of his immense concern for my safety. In all my born days I truly believe there shall never be a man as great and dear to me as Sherlock Holmes!

"My dear Holmes," I said quietly. "You look done in. It has been a long day. Let us turn in for the evening and we can start afresh on the diary tomorrow."

"Grand idea, Watson." He rose stiffly from the chair, a most grateful look upon his tired face. "Good night then." And he left me alone by the fire.

I knew I should follow suit, but I also knew sleep would not come regardless of the tiredness I felt. I wanted to continue on with the diary for the subtle bits of information had certainly piqued my interest. I also did not wish to intrude on Holmes's secret affair unless and until he wished it to be otherwise. Then again, had there actually been affair? Or was it just the fanciful inner longings of a lonely woman?

My pipe had gone out and I set it aside, content to stare into the dying embers and try to put the pieces of this information together in my head. But it appears sleep had snuck up on me some time during my contemplations near the fire for the following morning I was awakened early by a brisk shake on my shoulder.

"Watson! Watson! Are you all right old chap?" Holmes cried. "You have not retired at all man!"

I opened my eyes with a wild start to a sun filled room. The drapes had been drawn aside from the window earlier by Mrs. Garrett.

"You gave her quite a start, Watson," Holmes laughed. "Breakfast is nearly on the table if you wish to take care of your toilet first."

"Quite right, Holmes. Inform Mrs. Garrett I am sorry for that," I muttered. "I'll just be a minute." But it was a bit more than a minute. My old bones were stiff and my body sore from spending the night in an overstuffed arm chair and I knew it would take more than cold water across my face to get me going. It was almost a half hour later before I deposited myself at the table, muttering apologies to Mrs. Garrett once more.

"Feel up to a stroll the long way around to the beach?" Holmes asked as Mrs. Garrett poured steaming hot cups of strong fresh coffee.

"Certainly. The day looks to be a fine one," I yawned. "But I shall need two or three of these first," I said indicating the hot brew.

"Good. I've already breakfasted," he said as he drained his cup and stood. "You sit and enjoy and I shall take care of my bees. Then I shall fetch the diary and we will be off."

I did as he said and took my time enjoying the hot coffee and breakfast rolls and eggs provided by Mrs. Garrett. Just setting my napkin on the table, Holmes rounded the side of the cottage, caught my attention through the open window and I indicated to him that I was ready. We walked down the lane towards the cliffs enjoying the feel of a perfect Sussex day. The wind it seemed drew great energy from the ocean today. It was brisk and cool and held the smell of a storm in the air. Clouds sped across the sky building up slowly into jumbled billowing masses of ever darkening gray and would, by evening, be sending rain our way.

We strolled along the beach for a half hour or so and he related to me the strange case of the Lions Mane and how he had finally followed my advice and put it down to pen. "It is in my black box with the rest of the cases, Watson. You shall read them later, eh?"

We found our previous spot in the narrow hollow and made ourselves comfortable as once again he withdrew the diary from his pocket and handed it to me. "It feels strange to read of myself through another's eyes."

"But you've read my accounts of your cases numerous times, Holmes," I said, taking the diary.

"It's simply not the same, Watson." He shrugged his shoulders and gave me a weak smile. I smiled back and opened the book to read. Strange enough, I understood completely.

May 15, 1891

Several days have passed and my fugitive is healing now. His appetite is returning and it feels good to cook for someone once again. I found some large, heavy sticks and he is working at fashioning them into canes to help him walk. The leg pains him dreadfully for I can see it on his face. Today, I tell him I must remove the stitches, but he bids me to wait until my return from the village. And I agreed.

He has eaten nothing for supper and I am concerned. But it is time. I know he is brave and there is almost as much pain removing the stitches as putting them in. Sweat runs down his face and it is good he is lying down. I put a cold cloth to his brow and pull the last ones out. They were tight into the skin and they bled a little, but he did not cry out at all. He will heal. I applied a healing salve and fresh dressings and he lies breathing heavy.

For a long time he lay with his eyes closed and soon I saw that his breathing became more normal. He sat up then and, although he was pale, he smiled at me and said, "Now, Madam, perhaps I can partake of some of that delicious smelling stew still warmed at the fire."

I am glad.

May 18, 1891

Today he is very happy. His walking sticks are finished. They are not perfect but they will hold him. Very carefully he put his feet to the floor and tried to stand. I saw the pain on his face but he said not a word. Using the canes on both sides he walked with a heavy labor across the room. It is not a long distance but the sweat ran down his face and there was great pain on his face with every step. His left leg drags but it is to be expected. It will get better in time.

He reached the end of the room, stopped and leaned against the wall for some time breathing very hard. Wiping the sweat from his face, he began the walk back to the bed and nearly fell, catching his balance, but only just. When I rushed to help, the look on his face stopped me cold, so I held back and let him go. He is TOO proud, this fugitive.

May 20, 1891

The weather is good, then bad, but that is the way of it at the bottom of the mountains and the edge of the wild forests. I am busy preparing for spring planting and my goats are due soon with fresh young.

My fugitive is busy also. He is determined and although he is in pain, he walks about carefully inside the cottage. It is small and I can see he is full of energy that cannot be spent walking back and forth across the short distance inside.

Suddenly I hear a heavy noise and when I rushed inside he lay upon the floor, his canes leaning at the bed. I rushed to him and helped him up and to the bed.

"Monsieur!" I shouted at him. "It is much too soon to be so foolish. Put away your stubborn pride and realize a wound such as this will take long to heal no matter how much you wish it otherwise!"

"You are correct, Madam. I shall be more careful," he said between breaths.

I thought it was time. I said to him, "My name is Jeannette Dubois, Monsieur. And yours?"

He did not answer me right away but lay back with his eyes closed. Finally he said, "John... John Watson."

I looked up from the pages of the diary and threw a look of feigned askance at Holmes. He shrugged his shoulders as if in apology. "Sorry old chap. I certainly could not use my true identity if I were a fugitive, could I?"

His face held such a mischievous grin I could not chastise him for it. I shook my head at him and continued.

I know now he is a fugitive because Watson was the name he cried out so desperately in his fever. It could not possibly be himself he was crying out for! But I did not say so to him, of my thoughts. I thought it better just to let things be. It has been almost two weeks since I found him in my hen house. Now I have a name to call him. That is all I need.

May 21, 1891

Today I speak to John Watson. I tell him I know he is English but his French is very good. I tell him, I wish to speak English as well as he does French.

He has agreed to teach me and I am overjoyed! And so it begins. All that we say in French, he tells me in English and I repeat until it is always in my head. There are times it is difficult to understand his meaning, but he does not falter.

He is a gentle and kind teacher. He does not grow angry when I am having difficulty with his language and this makes me want to learn all the more.

May 25, 1891

Today is a beautiful sunny spring day, and John Watson tells me today he wishes to walk outside. I express my fears that perhaps it is too soon, the ground is uneven and he may injure himself again. But deep inside I know this is not to be true. I am afraid he will leave and not return.

But he is insistent and I cannot hold him back. He is not mine for me to do so.

He has gone out of sight and I am constantly looking out for him as I do my chores. He is gone for hours and the sun is getting close to the treetops. Soon it will be dark and I grow very worried. Even though he is not to be seen, I have prepared a meal for two. Hoping.

He has hardly spoken to me in the past few days. Just walks and walks and I could not help but wonder if he had gone. I sat at the table staring into my plate when suddenly the door pushed open slowly and he stood there, leaning against the frame looking pale and exhausted and breathing heavily.

"I am afraid you are correct once again, Madam," he said to me, his voice a wretched whisper. "I fear I have overdone myself."

He moved as if to fall and I rushed to his side. He did not push me away this time, but allowed me to help him. Together we made our way to the bed, my arm around his thin waist, his arm around my shoulder. He was chilled and shaking so I removed his shoes and wrapped the blankets quickly about him. After a while he began to breathe more normal and his color was not so white. He pulled himself up to sit and we ate our supper quietly this way. I did not ask of his disappearance.

It was a good meal. Chicken and dumpling soup with fresh bread. He asked for more and it was not long before I saw the color rising back into his cheeks.

He lay on the bed with his eyes closed. I thought he had fallen to sleep while I washed the dishes and put them away. But as I knelt to build up the fire he asked me, "Is there just the small village up the road?"

"Surely you did not walk the distance in your condition?" I cried to him. "The village is near three kilometers, Monsieur. It is no wonder you are all but spent. You shall be lucky indeed if the wound does not become infected once more."

"Yes, I shall be more careful from now on," he replied.

We went to bed that night, he exhausted from his walk to the village and I relieved that he had returned.

June 1, 1891

There has been little to write. John Watson has done as he said and is being very careful. He walks about the cottage and the yard only venturing a short distance into the forest. He has not returned to the village nor has he made mention of it again.

He follows me now, everywhere, writing notes on some paper I purchased for him. Notes. Always writing notes. He follows me to the hen house. Writing. He watches the goats and the milking, then follows me to the cold cellar. He is keen and quick. Asking many questions. Sometimes there are questions I do not know how to answer. His face is wrinkled with thought and I imagine him putting all the information into a tiny corner of his mind for later. He appears to me a very learned man but sometimes it seems to me he is learning more from me than I from him.

Once or twice I have picked up a discarded newspaper from the village on my trips to the market. He reads them over and over as if hungry for news. He does not throw them away.

He is quiet, this John Watson, but always I can feel him studying everything as if there were not enough time to learn all the world has to offer.

But he is also kind and gentle. His touch is delicate when collecting the eggs, yet firm and steady when milking the goats.

June 5, 1891

Today he wishes to help make the cheese. We went together into the cold cellar and for the first time we laughed. We poured the fresh goats' milk into the churn but did not have the old cover on securely. When he tried to turn it, milk flew into the air, drenching us both. We stared like silly fools at each other, the white milk dripping from our hair and face.

Then…suddenly…we laughed. We laughed until our cheeks were in pain and when we finally stopped, there was something changed about him.

I am having feelings for this John Watson, for he is a kind and gentle man. But he is also a fugitive and I know deep in my heart he must be on his way once he has regained all his strength and I will once again be alone.

Still…it does not hurt to enjoy his company while he is here.

"It appears, Holmes, that this woman is becoming smitten with you," I said when I looked up from the reading.

"Yes. It appears so."

"And? This did not bother you? Surely it was obvious the change in her attitude towards you. Even *you* must have noticed the signs."

"Watson, I will endeavor to explain to you what I have been unable to explain even to myself for all these years," Holmes said. He grew silent, closed his eyes and leaned his head back against the solid rock behind him and I dared not interrupt. I could tell by the look on his face that he was trying to think of the right words with which to explain.

"It was as if I were not me," he finally said. "As if I truly had become John Watson. Taking on disguises and the characteristics of others has always fascinated me and on those occasions which I employed those disguises I enjoyed playing the part...but none as much as John Watson. You understand, Watson, the disguises were intended to completely fool my adversary and they did, time and time again, and sometimes even my friends, eh? It was always a great art with considerable self-satisfaction to me at how completely I could disassociate myself from Sherlock Holmes."

He sighed with a great weariness here and stared at his hands as if embarrassed with having to explain. I remained silent and waited for I did not want to disrupt his thoughts. He finally continued. "It was different this time. Somehow, while playing the part of John Watson, I *became* John Watson; a strong-willed learned man intelligent and compassionate, a kind and gentle man ...." and here he stopped and looked over to me as though searching once more for the right words...."This was a new experience for me, you see, and I set out to test a theory..."

"Test a theory?" I exploded angrily upon him. "Of all the insane, idiotic, egotistical...test a theory? With a woman's heart? Were you mad?"

"The theory was..."

I was so angry and appalled by this turn of events I jumped to my feet and cut him short. I had never in my acquaintance of Sherlock Holmes known him to play such a loathing, despicable game of deceit. "Perhaps the fever *did* do irrevocable damage to your brain, Holmes!" I shouted, "for never, never would I have believed you to inflict any amount of such horrendous pain upon an innocent soul!"

Holmes himself now rose to face me for I had been shaking the diary in his face and towering over him in my anger. "Forget the theory, Watson!" He shouted back at me, his eyes flashing dangerously like the lightening overhead. "I cannot explain...not to you nor to myself. It all went wrong, don't you see? For the first time in my life those keen powers of deductive reasoning evaded me and I could not clarify nor rationalize my feelings. For the first time in my life I was falling in love with a kind, beautiful and wonderful person I knew I had no right to be with. I really *wanted* to be John Watson! That was the theory, *Watson*! To see if I could really change, to be more like you…to be…more normal…to start over…"

Silence. The silence grew between us like a giant wedge pushing between two pillars of stone. We stood on that sandy beach glaring angrily at one another while, it seemed our mood carried overhead. The sky had darkened considerably and suddenly there was a deep rumble of thunder amidst the blinding flashes of lightening in the air. I thought this was the first and only time in my life I believe Holmes had ever shown true anger. We stared for quite some time when his shoulders slouched and he hung his head to his chest. "Good lord, Watson. What have I done," he said, his voice a husky whisper.

Then all the anger that had welled up inside of me gave way and once again, I saw my old friend through different eyes. I heard and understood his outburst and I finally realized how difficult this entire episode of his life must have been. To be the great Sherlock Holmes, yet want to be…well…simply John Watson. My heart ached for this intellectually profound and brilliant man. "My dear friend," I said putting an arm about his shoulder. "There are no clues, no rational explanation for it. Love is the strangest disease in the whole entire world. And there is no cure. Nor any hope of ever finding one. It steals your heart like a ghost in the darkness and you are none the wiser. It makes you more happy then you could ever imagine while you are in it and tears you to bits when you have lost it. It is the most joyous feeling, yet the most dreaded. Holmes, I am sorry old friend for my outburst. I was out of line."

"No, not at all, Watson. I too, must apologize. It appears that there are times when there seem to be no words that can explicitly analyze one's feelings and that is especially true, or more importantly so, for someone like myself who thrives on the analytical. Feelings, emotions…well, it simply gets too complicated and it is for just this very reason that I have asked you to be my witness to this diary. You have been and always will be my dearest friend."

In all my years of having Holmes's acquaintance, I have never heard him speak anything of personal feelings of affection and I must admit, my heart swelled.

"Come," I said to him. "Let us return. I am sure Mrs. Garrett is wondering of our whereabouts. It is quite late you know, and the storm seems to be brewing frightfully overhead."

Holmes took the diary from my hand and replaced it in his pocket. Together we crossed the beach in mutual silence. The electrifying revelation from Holmes a few minutes ago still had my head reeling and it was all I could think of on our ascent up that treacherous path.

We had hardly settled before the fire in the study when the storm broke through the blackened clouds with a thunderous explosion. Holmes had ushered Mrs. Garrett on her way home as soon as we reached the house, wishing her to be home and comfortable before the storm arrived. We served ourselves lunch and I tidied up the table leaving the dishes in the sink for Mrs. Garrett in the morning as was her insistence. Holmes took a few minutes to steal a glance at his beehives. I heard him come in and close the doors just as the first large drops of rain slammed to the ground.

We settled once more in the study with a blazing fire in the grate while the storm raged overhead. I did not wait for prodding from Holmes but reached for the diary he'd placed on the table before us. I opened to read. He settled back into his arm chair and seemed to understand my eagerness to continue for he said not a word. What had transpired between us on the beach today had piqued my interest and I admit I am eager to read further. I turned the book towards the fire and began.

June 8, 1891

It is one month today that John Watson has come into my life and I am so happy. He moves about better now, only in need of one cane. There are still chilly evenings when the cool air comes down from the mountains as the sun sets and he says it pains him. But, just a little.

I am very busy now because I have the spring preparations. I have a large garden planted with vegetables and rows of berries and grapes. I put enough up at harvest to fill the long winter months for me and the rest I sell in the village market. This year promises to be a good harvest for the bushes and trees are already heavy with flowers.

He is a strange one, this John Watson. Of all the creatures on the earth, he appears fascinated by the bee. He watches them in my garden and follows them into the forest where he has discovered their hives. He has even brought back some of the fresh honey combs for me, his hand dripping with the sweet, sticky honey. And never a mark on him!

I remember the first time he hurried towards me, the sticky comb clutched in his hand. "Quick!

Quick, Jeannette!" He shouted to me. "Bring a bowl before we lose it all!"

It was much easier for us to laugh in each other's presence since the milk. And he was like a child, each day excited about new discoveries and knowledge. Yes. He is a strange man, this John Watson. But a wonderful man.

Today came as well as most. I gathered my things to go to the market and John Watson left for the forest to study his bees. I thought how strange that since his first time to the village, he has not mentioned it nor talked of going back there.

The market was very busy and I was gone the entire afternoon. Visitors and travelers from abroad sightseeing or simply lost, found their way to our quaint little village. We were all selling our goods.

My final customer was a man of the sea and wished to purchase my last round of goat cheese, but he did not have enough money and so turned to leave.

"Monsieur!" I called to him. "Wait. I see a book, just there inside your coat pocket. A trade perhaps?" I was remembering John Watson's fondness for reading and I thought perhaps this would be a nice gift.

He agreed quite readily and soon was off happily munching on the cheese. I packed up my empty baskets and the book into the cart and started home.

I have not seen such excitement on John Watson's face as when I gave him the book.

"Romeo and Juliet by William Shakespeare," he read aloud. "Tonight, Jeannette, you shall read to me of this Romeo and his Juliet. Your sweet voice is much more pleasing to the ear than mine."

I was so happy I felt my heart would burst, and could not help humming while I prepared the evening meal. It was certainly a good day.

That evening after the supper meal, we made comfortable by the fire, he lying on the bed and I sitting on a small stool nearby. I read Romeo and Juliet aloud.

Such a beautiful love story in such twisted times. I leaned my head against the bed and read, tears in my eyes at times. John Watson lay on the bed, his eyes closed, but listening. His hand which was resting near his side, slipped to the edge of the bed and I felt his fingers gently caressing my hair. I shivered inside at his touch but I dared not stop reading for fear he would stop. After a while his fingers froze when he must have realized what he was doing and I felt his hand pull away and he lay it upon his chest.

I continued to read as though nothing had occurred but I feared the beating of my heart gave me away.

I lay the book down, my mind racing at the words I had just read. "Holmes," I said, but he did not stir. I said it again, a bit louder. "Holmes!" and he slowly opened his eyes. "I think perhaps we should continue this tomorrow."

"Yes, you are right, Watson. It is enough for one night."

I put the diary on the table and we sat in silence puffing on newly filled pipes. The only sounds were the crackling of the fresh log on the fire and the thunderous booms amidst the pelting rain outside. There were so many questions to ask, so many personal questions and I did not know where to begin or if I should begin at all. After all, Holmes had called me here to be witness to the words of the diary and, I thought for as much respect as I have for the man, I should wait until he is ready to divulge the answers.

"We have had a good life all in all, eh Watson?" Holmes said, breaking the silence.

"Why, Holmes. You make it sound as if you are on your deathbed. You have fooled me too many times in the past and I certainly hope you do not wish to try again."

"No! No...not the deathbed, but when one reflects back upon one's life...all in all...it's been a pretty good turn."

"I expect so. There are moments I would prefer never happened," said I rubbing the bullet wound in my shoulder that ached intolerably with every change in the weather. "And then there are moments I wished would never end."

"Ahh...yes," he murmured softly.

I had been fondly remembering those years with my wife, Mary, and all the happiness we had delighted in by simply being in each other's company. Holmes, I assumed, was probably reflecting on the innocently sensuous scene painted by the words in the diary…or was there more? I began to wonder.

There was once more a long time of silence between us. I looked over to him sitting silent in the chair and saw that he sat with his eyes closed as he so often did, the smoldering pipe now rested in his hand. He sat still for so long I believed he had fallen asleep. I stretched and made to reach and remove the pipe and he stirred.

"I was just thinking, Watson," Holmes said in such a very hushed voice I had to strain to hear over the crackling fire. He cleared his throat. "I was just thinking, Watson," he said once more a bit louder.

"I thought you'd dozed off, my good man," I sat back and put my feet up on the ottoman once more.

"No, I simply took my time to reminisce in my mind about all we've been through, you and I."

I smiled at the thought. There were numerous cases we worked together. Or rather, Holmes worked and I bungled along. "I must admit I never knew what I was getting into when I agreed to share quarters with you at 221B Baker Street, that's for sure. And I also must admit, Holmes, I have never regretted that decision. Those were certainly fascinating and sometimes exciting times. You never ceased to amaze me with the simplicity in your deductions and yet I've always failed to grasp the concept."

"Perhaps it is because it was not as important to you as it was to me. You recall when we first met that day in the university laboratory? And later when I explained my theory of storing useless information in the brain and how it clutters and clouds that which is important?"

"I remember, Holmes. Only too well. I did not quite agree with you but then it was *your* theory and you were not looking for my agreement in the matter."

"But I have a theory on the theory. Look here, Watson, you failed to grasp the concept of simple deduction because you were too involved with your own personal affairs. Anything to do with an outsider was incidental to your existence."

"Are you proposing that I have been selfish in my own affairs, Holmes? Why, I was a practicing physician for many years and I took my patients very seriously. I…."

"Not at all, Watson, not at all," he held up a hand to quiet me. "What I am attempting to explain is this. You, as a normal intelligent human being, were so absorbed in the daily activities of your immediate you, that you failed to see that which was the obvious of others about you.

"I, on the other hand, found the study of other peoples' affairs intriguing, giving little thought to my own. This was especially true when it involved the criminal element. To channel all one's knowledge towards the study and application of apprehending that of the criminal element…to be able to study the criminal mind and then be able to stop the criminal action before committed. Or, more precisely, to be able to determine the action before the commission. *That* has always been the fire that blazed inside of me, Watson. But I have often found that in order to understand that aspect, one must understand the social, ethical and ethnic background of that criminal also. There are so many aspects of the criminal and the crimes that are yet untouched by today's police. It is certainly a matter of forensics for time and time again these elements are discussed but to no avail. They may be under discussion but there has been no set rule of application. Without that, the criminal element will continue to rule and win."

"You certainly have given this a considerable amount of thought, Holmes. Perhaps you should write more on the matter," I suggested. "Perhaps in the annals of science years from now students in universities the world over will flock to the study of your theories, your keen sense of deductions, your profound and diligent methods of gathering evidence and your intense analysis of the criminal mind."

"And where would you propose that area of study fall, Watson?" Holmes now leaned forward eagerly as the idea took hold. "Perhaps medical science for the study of anatomy is certainly necessary to determine the exact causes of death and, or quite possibly the methods applied. Or, possibly methods of gathering and storing evidence, for without that, there is no possible means of determining the true identity of the criminal or the crime. Then again, psychiatry such as Sigmund Freud has suggested. His study of the human psyche, he states, is altogether composed of the elements of a person's childhood. And the understanding of his youth would surely pre-empt a child from entering the criminal world if one could only..."

"Stop! Stop! Stop!" I laughed and held up a hand to stop the man. "I see you *have* been thinking about this far longer than just this evening."

"As a matter of fact, I have, Watson. And I need your help in the matter."

"My help!" I exclaimed. "Why, what help could I possibly render you in such a matter as this? This appears a bit out of my league of knowledge and realm of expertise, Holmes. I am now merely a retired physician. I do not even believe I was much help to you in all those cases we worked together. You are the key. You are the intellectual wizard when it comes down to it, my good man. I was simply…there."

"You underestimate your talents, my old friend. You are the key, not because you were simply…there…but because you served me with invaluable time and knowledge by being the buffer through which I could plausibly explain and work out my theories," he said, and I could see that old familiar air of excitement growing in him as in days of old. "Aside from the fact that you were instrumental in keeping accurate notes and clippings on each subject investigation making you an invaluable records keeper.

"We could work as a team as in the past, eh Watson? I have all the theories here," he pointed to his head, "but I require someone with a knowledge of practiced medicine and a practical nature to help me test them and develop them into a working study. I believe that not one course will do. There are so many aspects to consider that many courses will be required and a curriculum for each must be laid out in detail before I would be able to approach any university with this endeavor. I do not wish to study just the crime and its evidence, Watson. I wish to carry that to the criminal himself. I firmly believe that to know and understand why a person becomes a criminal may be the key to preventing that from happening in future generations. What say you, Watson? Are you up to the challenge?"

"My dear Holmes. You have never quested me a challenge that I have turned down before and although I am skeptical of my talents that you propound, I have no intention to do so now. Of course! I am at your service!"

"Good old Watson, I knew you would not fail me." He leaned back into his armchair quite satisfied that the issue had been settled.

"Holmes…eh…there is of course, the matter of the distance and time to travel. London to Sussex would…"

"Be a nuisance to say the least," he cut me off. "The thought had occurred to me, Watson, that you might consider taking up residence here."

"Here? With you?" I asked completely astonished.

"But of course. After all, we have shared quarters in the past and it did appear to work out admirably. There is the bedroom open which you currently occupy and I am quite sure it would take Mrs. Garrett no longer to prepare meals for two as for one. And, I might add, you may be the only human in the entire world who is able to put up with my idiosyncrasies and live to tell the tale. What say you to that, Watson!"

"I…I am quite taken aback, Hol…" but he cut me off once more, the excitement of the whole of his idea now overtaking him completely.

"I daresay it would work out admirably with you here. Our work would be long and tedious, sometimes actually boring because much of it would entail categorizing and working out the division of subjects into their proper area of study as well as their differentiation, but then again looking back over some of the theories we've tested, perhaps rather exciting."

The whole of the idea rushed from him and I thought he had uttered it so quickly he had hardly taken a breath. Then he stopped and a strange look fell upon his face. The type of look that comes about when one has a dawning of a sudden realization, and there appeared a crestfallen sadness.

"Or…perhaps I am presuming too much, Watson. The moment ran from me. It is so good having you here to discuss issues with that I did not think that perhaps you may not wish to leave the busy and exciting life of London for the quiet, lazy existence of the country."

"I should say you are correct, Holmes when you say you presume too much. However, it is too much on the one hand and not enough on the other."

"Forgive me, Watson, for now it is I who am confused. It is you who are speaking in riddles," he laughed.

"Here it is, then. You presume not enough in thinking I would not wish to leave London. Why, the very day I received your note, I was thinking on that very line but was in a dilemma. The small pittance of my military pension was at a loss to resolve that matter," I replied.

"And, on the other of presuming too much?" he asked.

"Too much in that we do not yet know the outcome of this diary. Perhaps events would precipitate changes neither you nor I will be able to control."

He looked at me through half slit eyes for quite some time puffing strong on his pipe. He blew the smoke thick then said quietly as though he'd forgotten the little book of memories on the table. "Yes…yes… you are correct, Watson. The diary." And we both stared at the book as if an answer were there waiting to jump out at us.

"Let us get on with it then. Read the next entry, if you will."

I reached for the book and opened to June 13, 1891, but did not read immediately. I said, "Holmes, whatever the outcome of the diary, I want you to know this. Ask me again when this adventure is over and I shall say yes."

"It will be good to have you, my friend."

I glanced at the faded lettering on the cover of the diary, and even though I wanted more than anything to continue, I decided enough was enough. There were revelations in Jeannette Dubois's words that were surfacing, subtly of course, but there nonetheless and I felt we needed time to absorb those words we had already read.

I put the diary back on the table and said, "It is late, Holmes. Why don't we retire and continue this tomorrow." I was pleased when he readily agreed. Even though I wanted to continue, in truth I did not feel up to any more surprises from the diary tonight. I had so much to think of and I feared sleep would evade me the entire night.

That night I lay in my comfortable bed and for the second night my mind raced over the events of the day. The diary's illusion to an emerging love affair....my move to Sussex...a possible partnership with Sherlock Holmes...busy and exciting life of London? Hardly! I drifted off to sleep thinking, Holmes was never more alive lest he was working a case. And I? I was never more so lest I was in his company. Exciting life of London? Hardly!

The following morning I was up late. Holmes had already sloshed through the mud of the evening's rain and had taken care of his daily ritual with the bees. I found him reading a newspaper. He was soaking up the warmth of the rising sun on the front garden terrace, its solar rays evaporating the puddles from the sodden concrete of the patio into a steamy mist as it dried. He looked up at my approach. "Well, well, well, old chap. You looked a bit done in last evening so I bade Mrs. Garrett not disturb you with her morning chores."

"Good of you, Holmes. I believe it is the clean country air. It fills the lungs with undisturbed fresh oxygen and tires one out completely by the end of the day," I laughed.

Mrs. Garrett arrived as if by magic summons with a pot of fresh coffee and a tray of breakfast toast and eggs. The diary lay on the table and we ate in mutual silence, the hum of the bees and twittering of birds providing a serenade of nature for our meal. It was a beautiful morning and I understood why Holmes rarely left his Sussex home. To live here would be a marvelous existence, but to live here with Sherlock Holmes would be extraordinary as well.

I picked up the diary from the table after Mrs. Garrett had cleared the tray and with a nod from Holmes, once again turned to the last entry. I immediately thought of the last entries read and wondered what new developments would occur today.

June 13, 1891

It is a beautiful day. The sun has finally come out just before noon following a morning rain. It glistens like shimmering diamonds on the spider webs intricately woven from branch to branch on the bushes and hangs in a million tiny colored droplets on the flowers of the late flowering apple trees.

I did not go into the village today because of the rain. And so it seemed that once the sun broke through the clouds both of us were anxious to be out and about. He, following the flight of the bees, and myself...

I do not know why but I simply spent the afternoon sitting on a small bench in the orchard among the trees feeling quite sad and lonely despite its beauty. For what reason, I cannot say.

After a while I saw him and watched as he drew near out of the forest. I knew by his look that he was once again making notes in his head.

He caught sight of me and waved me to him, and I smiled of course, and went. It was becoming too easy to be with him. But I did not care.

I approached him and saw that his clothes were wet from his walk into the forest. But he did not seem to mind or even notice. He was looking up into the last of the apple blossoms where the bees were in profusion buzzing about the petals.

"Look, Jeannette," he said with a great wonder in his voice. "See how they go from flower to flower extracting the nectars to return to the hive. It is a wonder to me how the flower is not disturbed and it still becomes an apple. And a more wonder yet how the nectar becomes the honey."

I looked to the flowers high above me and we stood close, side by side. He was tall and I was barely to his shoulder as we stood. He was rambling on about the bees, but I did not hear a word for in his excitement, his arm went about my waist and he drew me near. His face turned as he spoke and I could feel his breath upon my brow.

He looked at me then as he spoke but...suddenly he kissed me! A long, gentle kiss on my lips that I prayed would never stop. We drew apart and he stared into my eyes but for a moment, then looked down with embarrassment.

"I am so sorry. I do not have the right and should not have taken the liberty."

"But I have returned that liberty, John Watson, and there is no shame in that," I whispered to him.

"Still. I am sorry." He walked away quickly leaving me alone and I was once again more sad than ever.

I set the diary down and looked up. Holmes had risen abruptly, pushing the chair from the table and darted off down the lane before I had a chance to say a word. I was quite disturbed by the events of the diary and for the first time had absolutely no words to utter. I sat there thumbing at the cover of the little black book, so intrigued to read further but my loyalty to Holmes prevented me doing so.

He was gone for more than two hours. I was concerned, of course, but thought it best to let him sort his thoughts out alone. When he returned, I was strolling along the fence untangling some vines that appeared to creep along for miles. A senseless endeavor, to be sure, but I was too absorbed in my own thoughts to notice.

I heard a crunch on the gravel and I saw him from the other side of the fence as he walked slowly up the lane. The look on his face was one of the most discouraging sadness I have ever witnessed. His head was bent to his chest and his hands tucked into his pockets. It was a slow lumbering walk and I had the impression he did not wish to reach any specific destination as he plodded along. He stopped when he came to the gate of the fence and I saw his look was one of total bewilderment as if to say, ' How did I get here!'.

I was only a few feet away but I don't believe he even saw me or realized I was there. I stood silent waiting for him to do what? I don't know. Some time passed while he stared at the gate, but saw nothing. His gaze was fixed on some point far away and I knew he was at a moment in time I could never reach. "Holmes, are you all right?" I asked of him. His eyes moved slowly up to mine and as he set his sad gaze upon me he sighed heavily.

"I am supposing you would like an explanation, Watson," he replied dispiritedly.

"I was merely wondering, Holmes, what sort of game you were playing at, if truth be told."

He stood quite still and remained silent for so long I continued. "Look here, Holmes. This whole affair is of your doing and the choices you have made. I know love is…well…confusing to say the least. But I have been thinking a lot in your absence. And I really thought you should know. I am not here to pass any sort of judgment upon you, old friend. People make decisions according to the position they are in at the time. One can only hope the decision they chose is the right one. But life is a strange thing, my friend, because it is only in hindsight later that we can look back and clearly see whether it was right or not. Love is not something that can be analyzed or rationalized. There are no facts nor clues for anyone to follow. It just happens.

"Holmes, you need not explain anything to me. I have been in love and know that a man does the most adolescent things where the heart is involved. But I have also known the loss of that loved one and understand how it is to have a broken heart filled with regrets and to suffer over it interminably."

He spoke finally. "It was no game, Watson. I began my disguise as John Watson in the beginning only to play the part until such time I was healed and could be on my way. But the longer I was there the more I actually became John Watson. I had never felt so unencumbered of all my being before. It was as if there was a freedom there and I had been given a new soul.

"Her beauty. Her kindness. I have never seen such total devotion and unselfishness in a woman as there was in Jeannette Dubois. She was simply the type of woman one *must* fall in love with. And I wished it with all my new soul, Watson.

"Yet there were moments when the damnable soul of Sherlock Holmes burst upon me and I had to fight the John Watson soul by rationalizing that it would never work. It could never be, for deep down inside I knew in reality I was truly Sherlock Holmes. I am a man in need of constant learning and of continuous mobility and freedom. I knew it was wrong to take this woman's love because I knew deep down I could never change the real me. I could never be anyone else but me. Just me. It was a dilemma I had never faced in my entire life!"

"Excuse me, Mr. Holmes, but lunch is ready, sir," interrupted Mrs. Garrett from the terrace.

The sudden changes in Holmes I have never quite gotten used to. In an instant, a smile appeared on his face and he tightened up to the Sherlock Holmes I've always known and admired. "Very good, Mrs. Garrett. We shall be along shortly. Come along then, Watson. A hot cup of tea may be exactly what the doctor ordered, eh?"

We ate lunch in silence. What had transpired both in the words of the diary and the conversation and Holmes's revelations on the patio controlled my thoughts. I don't remember much of the lunch, only that I ate out of habit., and so, following lunch I suggested a break from the diary.

He readily agreed, stood abruptly, turned on his heel and went out to his precious bees. I watched Holmes's retreating figure and suddenly felt very tired. Sleeping the night with the windows open after the storm provided me with too much fresh air or perhaps it was the overwhelming events of the last few hours. I do not know. I went to my room intending to lie down and shuddered as the words of the diary came back to me.

Holmes's slowly emerging love affair was becoming too personal and I wondered if he would want to continue with the diary, if he would wish me to know all the events that had transpired. I instantly felt sorry for the man for obviously there was a loss here that he had hidden away for nearly twenty years. It must be heart wrenching to have to relive the events through the words of someone he loved.

Holmes, I saw from my French doors before lying down, had chosen the time to spend with the bees once more. His almost favorite place in all the world. I remembered as I lay down, thinking quite possibly this was so, for it must remind him of that period of his life when he felt most happy.

I napped for a couple of hours and when I woke much more refreshed, I found Holmes outside once more on the terrace. He set aside the newspaper he was reading as I opened the doors to the terrace. The sun was still warm and the breeze pleasing to sit in. I poured a glass of cold lemon mint tea and joined him.

"Ah, Watson, I was just thinking of you." He appeared in good spirits, the conversation of earlier seemingly nonexistent.

"Indeed. Good or bad."

"Good of course, old chap. I was thinking how all these years of our acquaintance I have truly underestimated you. You have an admirably keen insight into the human nature when it involves the sense of emotion."

"Why, that is good of you to say, Holmes."

"Quite. That is one more check on the chalkboard to have you join me. You must admit we make a good team. I may be the analytical and overly enthusiastic type where you offset me with your common sense and your sterling steadfastness."

"I have never doubted it in the least!" I exclaimed.

"Good. Good. It is settled then. I have the diary if you are ready for another go-round."

"Ready when you are," I said and he handed me the book. I looked at it thinking of the last entry I'd read and wondered aloud, "Holmes, are you sure you want me to read further."

"Watson, my old friend, I believe I know the balance of its contents. It is you I wish to hear and understand them. You know I have never been much of a storyteller. The words of Jeannette Dubois are much more effective at conveying what I cannot. Please. Read on," he said quietly.

"All right then." And so I began.

June 14, 1891

It is strange now. He does not wish to look at me and he makes excuses to be somewhere I am not. Today I will go to the village. I think, perhaps, we both need some time alone.

It was a good day at the market. I sold all my eggs and cheese and traded my last basket of eggs for a fish caught that morning by two of the village boys. They were so happy to bring the eggs to their mother and I was happy to have something fresh to prepare for supper.

He was sitting on the bed when I returned, reading the notes in his small notebook. He barely glanced up when I entered.

"Fresh fish, Monsieur Watson. Tonight you will taste the grand way the French prepare them," I said to him. It was a silly thing to say, but he immediately was interested and came to the sink.

I unwrapped the fish from the old newspaper it was in and I heard him gasp. I turned to him. "John Watson!" I cried out. "Whatever is the matter?"

"Nothing, nothing," he said rather quickly. "It is simply that I have never seen a better

specimen of fish before. But here...allow me...the paper. I am in need of some fresh reading material while you prepare the meal."

He swiftly took up the newspaper, rather too sharply, and went outside to read. I was surprised by his actions and walked to the window and saw that he had sat down on the steps to read it. He was so deep in thought he did not notice. But it was very strange. It was simply an old newspaper smelling of fish. I shrugged my shoulders and thought how desperate John Watson is for something new to read.

The day remained quiet. He read the paper and I saw it no more although I believe he did not destroy it. He was very quiet at the table and picked at his food.

"The fish, Monsieur? You do not like it?" I asked a bit upset.

"No...no..." he said. "It is delicious. I am sorry if my thoughts are far away." Then he finished his meal immediately and stood up, "I am going out for a walk, Jeannette. I need to think." The door slammed shut behind him and I began to cry. Things had changed since his kiss and I could not understand why. I had asked nothing of him.

He left and did not return until late. I had already gone to bed when I heard the door open. I was surprised, yet relieved, because I believed in my heart he had decided to leave. Then he came in quietly and sat on the bed.

"Jeannette!" he whispered in the dark to me. But I lay still by the fire and made as if I were asleep. I did not wish him to know I had been crying. He called out once more and when I did not answer this time he made ready for bed. I lay awake for a long time. When all was quiet once more I realized something was in that old fish newspaper that had sent John Watson back to being the fugitive. Then I also realized...now he would surely leave and I could not sleep at all.

June 15, 1891

Today is a strange day. He still has not spoken much to me. John Watson paces about the house as if he is searching for something. I see his eyes looking everywhere and he wants to say something, yet he holds back.

Finally when the breakfast was on the table he could hold back no longer. He blurted out, "What did you do with my old clothes? Those that I was wearing when you found me?"

"I burned them in the fire, Monsieur. They were beyond repair."

"The pockets? What of the contents of the pockets?" he snapped at me with great urgency.

"The pockets? Oh! Here!" I ran to the trunk beneath the window to get the envelope. "I had forgotten these things."

"And did you go through these things?" he asked staring when I took the envelope from the trunk and handed it to him.

"NO!" I shouted at him for now I was hurt and angry at his manner. As if accusing me of some wrongdoing. And he a fugitive! "I put them away and simply forgot about them. And you have no right to be this way to me, John Watson!"

And now, today, John Watson is different. He is eager and angry and when he tore the envelope from my hands I shrank back away from him. Without a word he went outside. He said nothing when he left and I stood there with my hands still in the air, empty, like a fool.

He did not go far. He sits on the bench near the garden and I watch him eagerly tear open the envelope. He must be pleased because I see a smile upon his face as he counts the English shillings inside.

He jumped up from the bench so quickly it startled me and I saw him go off almost running down the road. He went but a few feet...stopped abruptly and rushed back to the house.

It all happened so fast I was still standing like a fool near the trunk when he came bolting through the door. "I am off to the village. There is something I must do," he said.

He left in such haste he did not close the door. But he did not go far for once again he rushed up the stairs and into the room. "But I will be back!"

he shouted and this time he took the door and slammed it shut behind him.

And then he was gone.

I watched him rushing down the dirt road until he disappeared out of sight then I sat down and cried. My fugitive would leave and I was so foolish to think anything else of him.

It was some time before I finally came to myself and went about the house doing my chores. At first I was angry with myself for being so foolish, but when I thought of all the happiness he had given me for the past few weeks, I was very happy for that. I knew better. I had no right to expect any more. I did not expect him to return.

It was very late and darkness had come before I heard a step outside the door. When he entered I was so overcome with joy and relief I flew into his arms in tears.

He held me close and did not push me away but kissed my lips lightly then laughed at me. "My dear, Jeannette. Surely you did not miss me for such a short time as this? Come let us eat. I am ravenous and I see your plate is untouched."

He was so very happy as we ate and I did not know what to make of the strange changes in John Watson. I did not question what he had done or where he went but he said to me, "You will see, Jeannette. Soon things will change. They will change, Jeannette." And he smiled at me and kissed me once more.

He is not the most handsome of men, but tonight, when he looked at me and smiled in such a way, he was to me.

I do not know where he went or what he did and I do not care. Tonight he is once again the John Watson I know. We sat near the fire together wrapped in warm blankets and talked of dreams and plans for America. He speaks so freely of the both of us it as if we are one.

Suddenly he turned to me and said, "It will not be long now, Jeannette, for soon we will have money enough. Very soon. And I will buy us both tickets to go to America."

I felt as if in a dream and did not know what to say. I kissed him then and again he did not turn away. He kissed me in return and tonight! This night! This night he has made love to me and there are no words for me to describe. After, we lay together in each other's arms beneath the blankets until dawn.

I closed the diary very quietly and lay it on my lap. The sun was setting deep red beneath the horizon and as I looked across to Holmes, its roseate shadow revealed once more that he had traveled to a place so distant I knew I could not reach. Truth be told, the words of the diary left me in a somewhat embarrassing position. To read of a love affair of a close friend…a love affair so beautiful and captivating…I must say the diary put me in a most distressing predicament.

There are no words to say to a man when his love affair is so intimately revealed. And I had none to offer. I quietly rose from my chair rather stiffly, for we had been sitting the entire afternoon. He did not stir. I did not expect he would.

I left him there in the semidarkness, the diary in my hand. I did not wish to disturb him, first and foremost because I did not know what to say. Second, I felt it better to allow him time to come to terms with the words of the diary in his own time. As I looked back upon him from the doorway, I felt a terrible aching sadness deep inside of the tragedy of the diary. Already I could sense its outcome. I mourned the loss of his happiness almost as much as he surely must.

He did not appear for the evening meal and despite the sumptuous affair laid out for us by Mrs. Garrett, I must admit I hardly touched the food at all myself. She shook her head at me with some consternation but said she would put the remainder in the ice chest for later.

Holmes still did not appear even for the several hours I sat in the study alone. I had taken up one of his books from the shelf intending to read but I simply could not concentrate. I had placed the diary once more in its spot on the side table and it sat there still until he finally entered shortly before ten.

He came in silently and said not a word, but sat in the chair opposite me. He appeared exhausted and spent. He went to great lengths to fill his pipe and light it, then leaned back to close his eyes once more. I allowed the silence to fill the room. It seemed out of place to disturb it. It was sometime before he spoke.

"She was a romantic, was she not, my Jeannette?" he whispered.

"She certainly has a way with words, Holmes," I replied.

"Ah…yes, that she did, Watson. I believe she writes more eloquently than you. Her words are heart rendering and poignant. She could have been another William Shakespeare you know."

"I believe she certainly showed quite the talent in the diary, Holmes."

"You are wondering what changed. What happened."

"Something of that sort, yes." I replied.

"It was the newspaper."

"The newspaper?"

"Yes. The paper the fish was wrapped in. She did not see because she was too excited with showing me our supper. But when she unfolded the newspaper there it was staring right at me. Or rather, I was staring at me, Watson.

"The newspaper was weeks old and the headline read, "Famous Detective Dead - A Tribute to Sherlock Holmes, by Dr. John Watson," and there staring up was a large photograph of myself. I could not allow her to see that."

"Good heavens, Holmes, why ever not? It would have explained everything to her and solved all mysteries," I told him.

"That may have been so on the one hand, but on the other, it would mean that someone would know I was still alive. And don't forget, there were still Moriarty's cronies out there and I could not take that risk. Neither for her sake nor for mine."

"Yes. Quite understandable, Holmes, I do see that point. Still…"

"I read your account of my death and it was done with heart felt emotion. I thank you, my friend, for you gave it the appearance that I really was dead."

"That was simply because, my dear Holmes, I thought you really were."

"Don't you see?" He leaned forward earnestly. "That is exactly what I had been hoping for. I was healing and soon I could be off. I thought all that night of a plan and early the next morning I remembered I had had some money on me when we left the hotel in Reichenbach. I fear I was a bit abrupt with Jeannette because she misconstrued my entire meaning.

"We could not leave without money and I could not get money until I was able to wire Mycroft. The solution was so simple. I took the few shillings that were in the envelope and went to the village intending to do just that. I was not allowing for the fact that the village was so small and remote that there was no telegraph office, only a post. That set me back because I knew the post would be weeks waiting. But I was not disheartened, Watson. I sent my letter to Mycroft, under disguise of course, and made my return to the cottage. I had not counted on…on…well, the events that transpired," he said.

"It's the bloody human emotion of which I have had very little dealings with, Watson!" He exclaimed to me.

"It appeared to me you dealt with it quite well, Holmes old man," I said in a somewhat witty manner.

He gave me a look with a fire in his eyes and exclaimed, "Watson!" and I laughed. "I am sorry old friend. I do not wish to make light of your…um…the diary. But come man. It is rather comforting to know you can be as normal as the rest of us men in the world."

"Of course you are right. As John Watson I was in love with Jeannette Dubois. I had every intention of going to America with her. I had to give it a try, you see," he said.

"So, then what happened?"

"It appears that Sherlock Holmes began emerging after that point, Watson. It was as though reading your account of my death set me free so I wrote to Mycroft to give him instructions and to send me funds. For all accounts to the world I was deceased and so had no responsibilities or obligations to anyone. However, as John Watson, my responsibility lay with the foolishness of my heart. I was certainly in a dilemma. I became more restless and eager to be off, yet I wanted to stay. Besides, my wound would still not enable me that freedom quite yet. But I worked at it. I certainly worked at it," he finished, then grew silent, finally sitting back to stare into the fire.

"What say you we read a bit more of the diary, Holmes." When he did not agree or disagree, I reached for the book and opened to the next entry.

June 25, 1891

It is ten days since we became as one. He has not said much, but he remains happy and goes about taking his notes. It is much as before but I can see the restlessness building up in him. He hardly stays still. He walks and paces constantly.

June 28, 1891

I have examined the wound and there is no more to be concerned about. All that is left is a jagged scar. He is almost healed and rarely uses the cane. He goes to the village every day now and I can see him changing. Each day he grows more far away in thought. He paces always and soon I believe there will be a hole in the floor.

Today I did not go to the village but he did. I saw him on the road returning late. I watched from my open doorway with a growing sadness. He had a paper. A letter it looks to be, in his hand and was reading so intently he had stumbled. Upon catching his balance, I saw him look about quickly and tuck the letter inside his shirt. There is something he is hiding. His eyes are bright with excitement and he is whistling, yet he says nothing to me. I am afraid it will be time for John Watson to leave soon.

Evening came and we ate together near the fire. Later he turned to me and said, "Pack your things, Jeannette. You will be going to America just as you have always wanted."

"But I do not have enough for the tickets..."

He has put his hand upon my mouth to silence me. From inside the shirt pocket he has removed a large envelope but I know this is not the same paper inside his shirt.

"John Watson!" I cried to him when I looked inside. "These are tickets here...where did you..."

"Yes. I've thought of everything my dear, Jeannette. Train tickets to the coast then tickets on the ocean liner to take you to America."

"But there is only the one! You are not coming?"

He said to me. "Jeannette, my dear. Listen to me. I have received news in a letter along with the money here from my brother...yes...I have a brother. It is very disturbing news. It is a matter of which I must attend to. I will take care of this matter then I shall meet you in America."

"But I cannot leave without you. I must see to the affairs of my cottage and my animals. Oh, please, John Watson. Do not do this!" I cried and begged him but there was no changing his mind.

"I must go, Jeannette. I shall meet you in New York. You shall leave a letter for me at the

Ellis Island post. That is where the ships dock so that all foreigners must register. I shall find you."

I could see there was nothing I could say or do that would change his mind. I turned away from him but could not sleep.

I stopped reading from the diary and wondered aloud, "What on earth did your brother Mycroft tell in the letter that was so disturbing, Holmes? That you would even consider giving up your happiness with Jeannette for?"

"Good old Watson," Holmes said with an unusually gentle tone to his voice. "He wrote that your wife had passed away. It mortified me that at a time in your life when you needed comfort the most, I could not be there. It struck me what an ill opportune time it was to have feigned my death."

"Why, Holmes. Thank you for that. It was rather a bleak period of existence for me. First, my good friend Sherlock Holmes and then my wife, Mary. I ran the gamut of self-pity then anger and I felt I would lose my sanity. But I eventually came to myself and soon got lost in my work. I came to see that there were other people in worse situations than I found myself. At least I had wonderful memories of the two people in my life who meant the most to me."

"Ah...yes," Holmes responded softly. A silence grew between us and for a few minutes we both leaned back, both seemingly lost in our own memories. And then he spoke.

"Memories appear to have the same characteristics as emotions, do they not, Watson? Sometimes, when one closes one's eyes and reflects back on memories, sometimes they appear so real it's as if one can reach out and touch them. And it's the same effect as with emotions. While reaching out to grasp, to find something, anything, tangible, one's fingers still return empty."

"Extremely philosophical point of view, Holmes," I remarked, "and certainly one that will get no argument from me."

"I believe, Watson, the older one becomes, the wiser one becomes. What is your theory on that matter?"

"I've never really considered the subject too seriously, but if I had to say a word on the matter, I believe I would put it down to life's experiences. The more events one experiences, the more emotions one experiences. One makes choices based on experiences and emotions and later sees the outcome of the choices. One shares emotions and experiences with those close to them and it is as if they are one's own. All of which account for the basic fact that as one ages, one becomes wiser. All of that, no matter how trivial, Holmes, is stored somewhere in the human brain and brought forward to light without one even realizing it, thereby contradicting your theory of discarding or storing useless information in the brain. There is no such thing as useless information per se, but all information has some importance somewhere in everyone's life. It is simply the nature of mortal man for it to be so."

"Why, Watson, you've hit it all in a nutshell there. It's like taking a breath to tell oneself it does not matter and should be forgotten, for a breath is swift and gone to be replaced by another, but to try to forget, even the most trivial of information becomes as one's heartbeat. It makes no matter whether the memory is a good one or a bad one, does it. A memory is always there inside you and that's what keeps you alive."

"I believe you've spent your life as a detective, Holmes, but a great philosopher you could have been, *still* could be, you know," I said relighting my pipe.

"No, no Watson. Perhaps now in my old age that would suffice," he said leaning forward to rekindle his own pipe from my match. "But in my younger years I was too full of the need to know! The need to do. All my life, my time and energy have been in the pursuit of constant knowledge. Knowledge and analysis of the knowledge. And you, at times, Watson, have been instrumental in so much that that is why I have asked you to join me."

"I thank you most kindly, Holmes. And my statement still stands. I am at your disposal upon completion of this diary affair."

"Yes…affair," Holmes muttered and looked wistfully at the diary.

"Sorry old chap. Perhaps that was a poor choice of words."

"Not at all, Watson. It is late and I think we should call it a night."

"Right," I said and replaced the book on the table. "It has been a long day. Goodnight then, Holmes," I said and rose to retire.

"Watson!" he called out to me at the door.

"Yes, Holmes?"

"It *is* good to have you here, old friend!"

"It is good to be here…old friend. Goodnight." And I left him alone by the smoldering fire. Alone with his memories.

The following morning I awoke at what I thought was an early hour. I could smell the aroma of fresh baked biscuits and brewing coffee as I approached the kitchen. I discovered since Holmes had retired to Sussex that he'd made several excursions to the Continent, thus accounting for his newly acquired taste for coffee with his breakfast.

Mrs. Garrett was already busy in the kitchen when I popped my head in and inquired about breakfast A place was already set at the table and when she poured the coffee I asked, "There is only the one setting, Mrs. Garrett? Mr. Holmes is not breakfasting this morning?"

"Mr. Holmes has eaten and left more than an hour ago, sir, as is his custom," she replied.

"An hour ago?" I stammered and checked my time piece. "Why it is barely seven!"

"Yes, sir. Eats early he does, looks in on his bees then takes himself a stroll at the beach, sir."

"Well, thank you, Mrs. Garrett. This is a bit of news. I shall just have the hot biscuits and I'll join Mr. Holmes."

"Yes, sir."

I had forgotten of Holmes's odd habits and smiled at the thought of taking up residence here and how I would have to learn these all over again.

I ate the delicious honey sweetened biscuits and rushed down a couple of cups of hot coffee and thought it best I should be on my way without too further a delay. I usually

109

felt a great trepidation when faced with *The Path,* but it did not appear as treacherous today and I thought it was perhaps because I was becoming accustomed to its outlay. I was careful none-the-less and soon found myself standing on the sandy, pebbled beach scanning the area for any sign of Holmes.

My heart jumped into my throat when up ahead on the beach I saw a tweed jacket folded neatly atop a pair of black walking shoes near the rocks. I ran to them and braced myself for what I might find behind the large rock outcrop nearby. But as I approached, I heard the sound of water splashing and an utterance of a mild curse.

There behind the rock crouched in the water was Holmes. His trousers were rolled up past his knees and in his right hand was a large netted hoop.

"Shhhh, Watson," he whispered when he caught my appearance and he put a finger to his lips for silence.

There was no need to silence me for even had I wanted to say something, I could not. Out of breath from the run, I was also too surprised to think of anything to say at the sight that lay before me.

I watched now with interest, as my earlier fear subsided, while he inched forward in the water and slowly lowered the net. There was more patience there than I could ever muster for it was some minutes before the whole of the net went into the water. He dragged the net forward and with a sudden jerk that startled even me, he wrenched the net from the water spewing water in all directions.

"Supper! What say you to this, Watson?" He laughed, struggling to hold the net while a large fish thrashed angrily inside.

"Well done, Holmes, well done! But don't you think a hook and line would have been more appropriate?" I laughed.

"Not in the least. This follow has been eluding every conventional means of fishing I have tried. He is a wise one and I had to bow to the unconventional to trap the sly villain!" He spoke while exiting the water. "It seems a shame to have caught him in such a fraudulent maneuver, but I have waited long enough to have a taste of this fellow on my supper plate." He twisted the top of the net tight and set the fish in the shallows until our return. Then he sat on the beach and bared his face to the sun while he allowed his feet to dry before replacing his stockings and shoes.

I looked around at the scenery about me. It was peaceful and quiet here, close to the small hollow. The breeze was gentle having been calmed by its route through the natural breaker of standing stones set against the ocean. The water too, was calmer here, as it lapped with lazy slaps against the rocks. I gave a heavy sigh, a sigh of calmness and serenity and said, "I can certainly understand why you come here, Holmes, despite the path. It is a wonderful spot."

He'd replaced the stockings and shoes and now stood to unroll his trouser legs. "Yes it is, Watson. Quite the difference from all the children's noises and horse and carriages clacking down the streets of London, isn't it? But of course, now there is the automobile, too."

"Do you miss it?" I asked rather abruptly. He took some time to reply. His gaze went out past the small cove and I saw a faraway look enter the gray-blue orbs as if stretching to see across the ocean, across the miles, across the memories.

"Yes, sometimes I do. In London? On all those cases? I never felt more alive. I thought that was what my life was meant to be. I was thrilled and excited by it all, even allowing for those mundane days when I resorted to the use of drugs to stimulate my senses. To which I owe you a debt of gratitude, by the way, for insisting I discontinue that practice. Life is and can be most stimulating all on its own, if one seeks to find it."

"You are so very welcome in that regard, Holmes. And now?" I prodded.

"Now?" he turned to me, a most horrendous look of crushed defeat upon his sad features and said, "Now it appears I am simply an old man with hidden secrets and memories just like any other."

"But it need not be this way, Holmes? You were the best! Still are in my book and you still have so much to offer!"

"Do I Watson? How can I offer my assistance to someone else's life when I have made such a bungle of my own? Do you think anyone in the public would even ask for my assistance should this diary affair come to light? And it may come to light in a manner which may cause alarm in some quarters of London."

"Good lord, Holmes!" I shouted at him. "This is utter nonsense the way you talk! In the twenty or so years since this affair occurred you have managed, quite effectively I might add, to come to the aid of many distressed citizens in many countries. There was never a bungle there and there is no bungle here, Holmes. There is just the story of two people once in love and a tragedy that befell them. There is no bungle in that, Holmes!"

"Yes...like Romeo and Juliet, eh Watson?" he smiled, but his eyes still reflected a great sadness.

"In a way, yes. The situations and circumstances may be different, but a tragic love story is a tragic love story, no matter in which time it falls. And furthermore, this instance in your life in no way reflects on your astounding abilities at all, Holmes. Come man...look back and think again on the countless cases you have solved and the numerous people you have set to right. Why, the streets of London would not be half as safe had you not rendered your services to make it so."

"You may be right, my friend," he replied turning from me, and once again I had that old familiar feeling that the conversation was over and he did not wish to discuss it any further. I shook my head and opened my mouth to say something for I wanted to bring the matter of the diary to a head, but he continued, "Let us make ourselves comfortable. The diary is here in my pocket." He handed it to me and said, "Would you read further." I was slightly put out at his curt dismissal of the subject but now thought better than to try to continue the conversation. I did not wish to alienate his openness towards me because now I felt he needed my help more than ever.

We settled once more on the beach inside the calm of the hollow and I opened the diary once more. I was growing more concerned as each day passed but thought it best to keep my concerns to myself. At least for now. He apparently felt an urgent need to continue with the diary and so I read on.

June 30, 1891

My John Watson is once more a stranger to me. I do not know his mood from one minute to the next. He rises early each day and is gone. Sometimes he returns from the forest. But most times he is returning from the village.

The time draws near when I must travel by the train. He will not ride with me, he tells me, for my own safety. I sense more and more something is wrong and there is a danger for John Watson.

I have sold my animals and a local man from the village has made a generous offer on my cottage. We will exchange the ownership and then I will have no choice but to leave. But there will be money enough to make a new start in America. And that makes me happy.

He has purchased more paper and pen for I see him writing and writing more. He is quiet now and spends his time away from me. I fear he is truly a fugitive from the law that has stolen my heart. But there is no turning back now.

July 8, 1891

It is now two months since John Watson has come into my life. I do not know how I ever lived without him. He has paid a man to take us by cart to meet the train. I am confused.

I am sad to say goodbye to my cottage for there were many happy memories here. With Josef, my husband, and now with John Watson. I do not wish to go.

But, I am also happy and excited to be off. I dream of a new life in America and John Watson to share it with me.

We have reached the train station but must wait. The train is late and it is very chilly and rainy. John Watson has put his coat about my shoulders to keep me warm. We sit on a bench inside the station together. His arm is around me holding me close and I am happy for this moment.

A man walked by reading a paper and John Watson jumped up to follow him. I heard him ask, "Excuse me, sir. That is a telegram? Is there a telegraph office here?"

The man answered, "Yes. It is less than one kilometer in that direction," and he pointed out the window.

He rushed back to me and I can see the urgency upon him. "Jeannette, I must go to the telegraph office and send a wire. I will be back as soon as I can!"

"No, please! Do not go! The train will be here soon and I do not wish to leave without you!" I cried.

He put his arms around me and held me close, so close I could hardly breathe and at that moment it felt as if my heart would break for I thought that this would be the last time I would see John Watson. Then he put his hands to my face and kissed me and said, "I must do this, my love. You must understand there are events of my past I must deal with. You will take the train and then the ship to America as planned. I WILL COME."

"Please, please...," I was crying and did not wish to let him go.

"Jeannette," he whispered my name so softly I held my breath to hear. "I have never known such happiness as I have with you. You must believe me. I will come."

And then, at that moment, I knew he would. I wiped my tears and said to him, "Go then if you must. You have already stolen my heart, John Watson. And I shall wait for you."

He made to leave but I called him back from the door. "Wait! Your coat! It is raining and cold and you will need it. I will be fine."

He reached for the coat and in his haste of putting it on, the old newspaper of the fish fell to the floor. He did not notice for the door was closing behind him before it even touched the floor.

I picked up the paper and returned sadly to my seat on the bench near the window and watched him hurry away until he was lost in the rain out of sight. The train would be arriving soon and I did not wish to cry again so I thought to read the paper and wait for John Watson to return.

Some of the pages had been destroyed by the fish but...oh what a shock! I opened the paper and saw John Watson staring up at me! My hands trembled so badly and my heart raced in my breast I felt I would surely faint. It was a few minutes before I could look at it once more and then I read , "Famous Detective Dead - A Tribute to Sherlock Holmes, by Dr. John Watson". I read eagerly the paper and could not believe it. My fugitive was not John Watson, but this famous man Sherlock Holmes! I cannot say what I did for the next few minutes. I did not hear the train pull in and I did not see the people moving past me to board.

A porter touched me lightly on my shoulder. "Excuse me, madam, but I believe this is your train." I folded the paper to me and boarded the train. Alone.

"Holmes, might I ask what the devil was so important at the telegraph office?"

"I had finally found one, you see, Watson. I went to wire Mycroft that I was returning and that I would wait for his immediate reply. It should have only taken a few minutes for the wire, but it seems Mycroft was in a meeting with the king and could not be disturbed."

"What on earth were you returning to London for if Moriarty's cronies were still about?"

"For you, Watson. I wished to be sure you were all right dealing with the death of your wife so soon after my own."

"Holmes! I am extremely flabbergasted! You put my concern above your own safety? That was indeed a most foolish thing to do!" I exclaimed at him. I was also so touched and moved by this gesture I had to turn my own head away that he would not see my eyes bright with tears.

"It would have been in disguise, my friend, and you would not have known unless there were drastic circumstances. But Mycroft's telegram stopped me cold."

I blinked back my emotion and said, "And how was that?"

"He wrote that my rooms at 221B Baker Street had been broken into and gone through very thoroughly. There was a terrible mess, he said. Obviously whoever did it was looking for some indication of where I might be if were still alive.

"No, Watson. I am truly sorry for not returning in your time of need, but Mycroft's letter meant someone still did not believe in my demise and I would have to stay 'dead' a bit longer."

"Quite understandable, Holmes, no need for an apology. Your thoughts are more than sufficient. Still I do need to ask what happened then? At the train station, I mean."

"It took longer than anticipated and I ran back immediately to the station hoping it had not yet arrived, but that was not to be. I was so very angry with myself at the moment. With my foiled attempt to return to London, I could have accompanied Jeannette to America after all.

"The train had come and gone and there would not be another for three days. I could do nothing but wait. I found lodging in the town and busied myself until the train three days later. I had hoped once more, that perhaps the ship would be delayed, but ships rarely are. She left dock on time and I missed Jeannette once more. My passage was not until two more weeks so once again I busied myself until my ships' departure. But we are getting ahead of the diary, Watson," he stopped.

"Shall I continue then?"

"Why don't we take our thrashing scoundrel there to Mrs. Garrett," Holmes said indicating the fish in the net. "We will continue this after lunch, shall we?"

"No argument from me, Holmes." I rose and handed him the book and he put it away once more in his pocket, and once more I detected a minute hesitation as his fingers caressed the cover. Quickly, he retrieved the net from the shallows and we walked casually back across the beach, speaking of trivial events while the fish trashed about angrily in the net behind us.

Once back on the lane, the wind grew brisk and I pulled my sweater tight about me. Holmes deposited the fish with Mrs. Garrett and as lunch was more than an hour off, we decided to take a short stroll down the lane.

Here he pointed out to me his nearest neighbor, Harold Stackhurst, who ran a coaching establishment called The Gables. They were acquaintances, he said, with Stackhurst being a straight forthright fellow of impeccable integrity and congenial enough to pop in upon without an invite. It was good to know that Holmes had acquaintances here, for

I was beginning to fear the solitude was affecting his rational judgment.

The conversation on the beach came back to me and I wanted to confront him once more but I knew this was not the time. His mood was cordial now and I did not wish to disrupt that with the thoughts of self-doubt he had expressed to me earlier.

I was bothered by this for never in my whole acquaintance with Holmes had there ever been the slightest trace of doubt in anything he said or did. He was a man of great knowledge and spirit, full of determination and control. It seemed, as we read further into the diary, I could see this spirit ebbing away from him, I could feel the control slipping from his grasp. I did not know how, but I vowed I would do whatever it takes to bring Sherlock Holmes back to his former self. But he brought the issue to head sooner than anticipated.

"You are lost in thought, Watson. It is on my account, eh?" he asked as we approached the gate to his villa.

"I was, Holmes, and yes it is. Excuse me for being so bold, but I believe you are slipping. I recall not so long ago, you would have told me exactly what it was I was thinking."

"And you feel that it is of course, due to the diary."

"Yes. Always that confounded diary. It appears to have taken control of you, man. You are not yourself. If there is that much concern, we could burn it in the fire and none would be the wiser!"

"I know you say this out of concern for me and I am grateful for that concern. But the diary is all I have left of Jeannette Dubois and right now, it is something I do not wish to destroy. I have destroyed so much I simply cannot do one more. Besides," he stopped to hold the gate open for me, "once I missed the train, I have no knowledge of what befell Jeannette....at least not until I reached Ellis Island in New York...that is another read, eh Watson? Let us enjoy our lunch and as the weather is still rather pleasant, we shall start afresh on the diary on the terrace."

We sat together at a quiet lunch, both of us lost in our own thoughts. The subject had been approached but not cleared and I was sure it must be brought up again some time soon. How I would bring it up again, I do not know.

He picked at his food and after barely touching anything on his plate, he shoved it aside, rose without a word and went outside. I finished my meal and made it a point to let Mrs. Garrett know how greatly it was appreciated, despite her chagrined look at his untouched plate.

I found him sitting on one of the rattan chairs on the terrace smoking his pipe. His closed eyes gave every appearance that he was sleeping, yet I knew better. Perhaps it was after all these years of having his acquaintance that I finally was able to come to some of my own deductions. I could tell by the manner in which his head was thrown back against the chair that he was in deep thought.

I said not a word, but sat opposite him and lit my own pipe and we smoked in silence for a while. Thinking back of Holmes's own admission that from this point on in the diary he was as in the dark as I, my curiosity got the best of me and I finally asked, "Shall I continue this Holmes?" indicating the diary he'd placed on the table in front of him.

"Please do, Watson...please do."

July 15, 1891

I do not know how I managed to get through the next few days. They are a blur to my memory. It seemed I traveled on the train endlessly and then I was on the ship. I do not remember leaving the train. I do not remember boarding the ship. But there I was. For some days I stayed in my cabin crying all the time and feeling too sorry for myself to leave. But the day came that I knew I must.

It was a calm day, a blue sky overhead and I soon found myself standing on the deck leaning on the rail looking out at the ocean. It stretched for kilometers in every possible direction and I felt surely there was no end. It was so beautiful and peaceful one could hardly feel the ship's movement on the water and it was as if we were standing still in time. A woman came and stood beside me and asked me my name. "Jeannette Dubois," I told her without even realizing I had spoken.

"My name is Michelle Dutton. Come with me, Jeannette Dubois," she said putting her arm through mine, "you look to be in need of some fresh hot tea." And she led me away. I heard her

voice then. It was with a French accent and we broke out in French so rapidly others stared. We laughed like silly school girls who had found a lost friend. It was so good to laugh once more.

She was very nice, this Michelle Dutton and we became friends on that long ocean voyage. She was French also, but had married an American, or would soon marry him. This she did by an advertisement in a newspaper. I was shocked but she said it was her only chance to be out of France and into America for a new life as he had paid her fare to cross. Then I could understand it, for I too was going to a new life and my fare had been paid also by a stranger. But it was a new life I wished with all my heart would be shared with John Watson. I did not speak to her of John Watson. I did not wish to share him with anyone.

July 19, 1891

Today is not so good. There is a fever on board the ship and many people are ill. I have volunteered to help in the sick area for one of those is my good friend Michelle Dutton. I have felt the uneasiness in my stomach also, but do not have the fever and so wish to help.

It is a bad fever and she lies sleeping very restless. I sit by her side all through the day and have brought my old newspaper to read. I do not know why, but once more I opened the pages to read again of Sherlock Holmes. There is a woman from England in the next bed and she speaks to me, "I see you were one of his admirers also, madam."

"Admirers?" I asked of her. My English was still not so good but I understood most of what she was saying.

"Why yes, dear, of Sherlock Holmes. I am from London, you see dear, and let me tell you, that man was the greatest detective that ever lived. And a kind man. But also a very strange man."

"Strange? Was?" I did not understand this and turned to look upon her. She was an elderly woman with graying hair tied up in a bun tight to her head and brightly painted cheeks and lips and did not appear to be ill in the least.

"Why yes, dear. He worked with the police and Scotland Yard of London many times. His cases were published by his good friend and partner Dr. John Watson. Why, I do believe if it were not for him, England would be overrun with criminals! He had a nose for the criminal that one did! Many are the folk who cried when Sherlock Holmes was murdered!" she cried.

"Murdered!" I whispered.

"Why yes, dear. Murdered. You see, there was a very bad man operating in London by the name of Professor Moriarty. He was as bad as they come and Sherlock Holmes was hot on his trail, as Dr. Watson would say."

"Moriarty," I said and suddenly the name came back to me and I realized he had been crying out in his fever to warn his friend Watson of this Moriarty. And now things began to make some sense to me.

"Why yes, dear. Moriarty. It was him that murdered Sherlock Holmes!"

"Murdered!" I whispered once more.

"Why yes, dear. Murdered. You must pay attention, dear. In that article so eloquently written by Dr. Watson, both Sherlock Holmes and Professor Moriarty were fighting somewhere in Switzerland and fell into this great canyon or something of water with no bottom. Fell to their deaths they did and nothing of them has ever been recovered. After all, how could it be when there is no bottom and one cannot possibly get down to retrieve the bodies and even if he survived the fall surely...."

I could stand it no longer and left running from the room while she was still talking on and on behind me. But I did not care. I had to leave, to get out. To get some air and to think. I ran out onto the deck but it was too crowded there with people. I flew by them and went below to my cabin to be alone.

July 22, 1891

I have been ill but not with the fever. I am much relieved when the following day I returned to Michelle Dutton and the gray-haired English woman has gone. I will stay all day today and sit with Michelle Dutton because she is not doing well and I know she will not live to see America.

I think constantly of John Watson. He is never far away from my thoughts. Michelle Dutton is sleeping now and I feel as though I am suffocating. I must leave her for a moment. I returned to my cabin and pace the floor like John Watson.

Tonight I am in my cabin and I do not like being alone. But I have thought of something.

This John Watson of mine. He is the greatest detective, this Sherlock Holmes. He is pretending to be dead to escape this Moriarty, I think. And then it comes to me. The reason for his strange behavior. I know now, that my life with John Watson can never be.

As John Watson he has loved me with all his heart, but as Sherlock Holmes, he needs his freedom and I know this in my heart. Sherlock Holmes is a man of many talents and great energy. I cannot hope to hold his love when he is already in love somewhere else. Deep in my heart I know that in order to give Sherlock Holmes back his life, I must let go of John Watson.

It was then the idea came to me. It rushed upon me so quickly I did not think of what would happen should I be caught. I have gone back to my friend Michelle Dutton. She is unconscious with the fever and does not see what I have done.

I know it was wrong, but sometimes there are unpleasant choices one must make.

When there was no one about, I removed her ticket and her passage packet from her handbag and replaced it with mine. I did it quickly for I did not wish to be seen. Then I sat with her until morning. Then she died.

July 23, 1891

They have taken away the body of Michelle Dutton and cleaned the bed. I am in her room now because I carry her identity. My heart aches for her for she was my good friend. I miss our conversations and the way she giggled over silly things. She was a very sweet and kind person and it was a shame there was no one to say so. But I will always remember her in my heart and my prayers and I send many thanks to her soul for the new beginning she has allowed me.

I know this choice of my life will be forgiven. I must give Sherlock Holmes back his freedom, for without it, he would wither as the flowers from the mountain snows. I also know, deep in his heart, Sherlock Holmes could never love me as John Watson has.

"My God, Holmes, why on earth would she do such a thing?" I cried.

"I do not know, Watson, but we shall finish inside. It has grown quite dark and I see you struggling to read without the light," he said.

"Mr. Holmes, supper is on the table, sir. And if that is all, I will take my leave," Mrs. Garrett announced from the door when we entered the house.

"Very good, Mrs. Garrett. We were just on our way. Come, Watson. A good meal, a good smoke. And the evening will be set."

"Here, here," I said and tucked the book into my pocket. I was hoping he would have more of an appetite now than at lunch because Mrs. Garrett had labored to prepare his thrashing scoundrel. We washed and sat down to a beautifully prepared fillet of breaded fish served with a touch of lemon and rice.

"You certainly found a gem of a housekeeper in Mrs. Garrett," I told Holmes while we cleared the dishes to the sink.

"Yes, she came highly recommended and I dare say I could never ask for better. She is a terrific cook, a great housekeeper and she knows to keep her tongue in the village of my affairs here. She certainly is a gem, Watson."

We made our way to the study and sat lazily puffing on our pipes for quite some time. I patted my pocket and I felt the diary there. I withdrew the thing and made to put it on the table.

"Might as well get on with it, Watson," Holmes said. "There can't be much to the telling now."

And so I opened the book to the mark and began. "There is no date here, Holmes. It simply starts at the middle of the page." And so I read…

It has been several weeks on the ocean and today I go to the deck amidst the cheers. There ahead of us is the bright shining Statue of Liberty I have read about and so longed to see rising in the harbor. She is beautiful, her great torched arm raised to greet us. She is the most beautiful face I have seen in my life!

I have made a decision to leave this place and travel to the west where I am hearing there are mountains and rivers and land for everyone. I wish to settle near them for they will remind me of my own home so far away.

I feel sorry for the man my friend was to meet and marry, but I cannot worry about him. I will keep the name of Michelle Dutton and using some of the money my John Watson has given me, I have purchased a ticked on the first train going west. I do not wish to be constantly reminded of all that has happened to me, yet, I do not wish to forget any of it either.

I cannot begin to write of the love I have for John Watson and will always have. He will hold a space in my heart no other will ever enter. I know my decision is the right one for he is a man that cannot be held down. I will tell my children of this, only when they are ready. I know now why I was ill but with no fever. And now it is all the more important of my decision, for I could never tell John Watson that I carry his child.

I will write no more in this diary. There is too much heart break here.

The shock of the words in the diary sent my head reeling and I almost dropped the book from my grasp. Holmes had risen from his chair to stand before the fire, his back to me. I stared at him for some time, the words I had just read seemed to still be echoing around the room.

"Holmes. Did you ever know?"

And now that I eagerly awaited an answer, the room seemed to grow deathly still. Even the crackling of the fire on the grate was muted and distant and muffled as if we had been thrown back into another dimension. A time that seemed an eternity but was in reality a few seconds before he answered and when he did his voice was distant and trembled.

"No...no Watson. I never knew. Until now when the words of the diary took my breath away. A child! A child, Watson! *ME!*" He turned to look at me and by the bright yellow glow of the flames I saw upon his face a look of strange terror amidst the shallow tinges of white that I thought I would never live to see upon the face of Sherlock Holmes.

"But surely, Holmes. When you went to America. Did you not make any attempt to find her?"

"But of course I did, Watson! Don't be a fool!" He shouted. He turned to pace with an urgent surge of energy and the words spewed from his mouth so quickly I had to lean forward to catch them all. "My ship arrived two weeks after hers and the first thing I did was to go to Ellis Island. I went to every registration table but no one had an entry for Jeannette Dubois. I was nearly out of my mind with worry until one of the clerks suggested I check the ship's passenger manifest.

"I was so out of my mind with concern I failed to see the obvious, Watson. I could not even think."

"Yes. I understand now how you came to your theory of simple deductions. When one's mind is cluttered and clouded with too much concern over every day personal matters, one cannot see the obvious. It all makes sense, Holmes."

"Exactly, Watson! And here, in this instance, I was no different. I immediately went to the office of the shipping line and explained my situation. The clerk there was most helpful and bade me come in to speak with the office manager. A Samual Cotton by name. He explained to me of the fever on board the ship and that Jeannette Dubois had been one of the five passengers that had died at sea.

"I remember jumping up from the chair and shouting at the poor man, "You lie! This is impossible! This must be a mistake. But it was not a mistake, Watson. He pleaded with me to calm down and he brought out and showed to me the records of the ships log and a certificate of her death. It was all there, her name, France where she was born and America where she was destined. She never made it there, Watson. Or so I thought until today." He stopped once again at the fire with his back to me and hung his head to the mantle. I was immediately filled with such sorrow for him. It was as if his heart was breaking all over again.

"What happened then, Holmes?" I quietly asked.

He began to pace the room again and run a hand through his hair over and over and said, "I was crazy for a moment and I thought of you losing your wife and I knew how it felt to be once more alone. Alone and vulnerable. I had never felt myself vulnerable in my life, ever, Watson. It was a shattering experience for me. I walked the streets of New York until I could walk no more, then found a room. I sat up the night and by morning I knew what I had to do."

When he did not continue I prodded. "And that was?"

"I knew I would never allow myself to be alone or vulnerable again. I would get myself back on with my life and get on with it. To get on with my life as Sherlock Homes, after all who did I think I was fooling? I could never remain John Watson. It was a disguise I played and played only too well. It nearly tripped me up. But I was no longer John Watson. I was once again Sherlock Holmes. No obligations…no responsibilities. I set myself to do what I had planned all along. Lose myself until such time as was safe to return to England.

"I mourned her, Watson. With all my heart I mourned her. And before I returned here to London, I made a trip to her small village and back to the cottage. The place had not changed much, except that it was deserted then. I walked through the cottage and sat near the fireplace on the floor where we used to sit together and the memories flooded my heart. I sat on the bench in the orchard where she loved to sit on a bright, sunny morning and listen to the birds. There were flowers growing, now wild from neglect. It was a silly thing of me, but I picked them and lay them on the bench for her. I said my goodbyes then and I made a promise to both Jeannette and myself that I would never allow another woman to enter my life as I had Jeannette Dubois. Then I left and never looked back."

I rose and went to him near the window where he had finally stopped his pacing and was staring out into the darkness. I lay a hand to his shoulder. "Holmes, it is near one in the morning. I believe we have had enough. "

"That is so, but I am afraid now sleep will evade me altogether."

"Yes, I feel the same but let me ask what you would prefer, my old friend. Would you rather be left alone or wish my company still." He thought for a moment before answering, then said,

"I have been alone much of my life, Watson and would rather prefer you stayed."

"Right then. I shall go brew up a fresh pot of hot strong coffee while you put another log on the fire."

When I returned, the fire was blazing nicely and Holmes was once again sitting in his chair. I poured the coffee and we nibbled on the left over sconces I'd found in the ice chest and included on the tray with the coffee.

"One would think as one grows older, that there could never be surprises in one's life anymore," he sighed.

"Yes, but, when one lives an adventurous and intriguing life such as yours, surely, Holmes, there have got to be surprises. Even you could not discount that."

"But a child, Watson. Me!"

"It sure boggles one's mind does it not," I said.

"And how so?"

"Well, look at it head on, Holmes. You have never been...well..been any of the sort inclined towards women. And now, of course, I understand completely why."

"Ahhh...but Jeannette was not *just* a woman, my friend. I allowed her into my heart as *THE* woman. And once that spell was broken and I found myself Sherlock Holmes once more, I vowed that would never happen again. I do not enjoy being vulnerable, Watson. And that woman made me most vulnerable. I lost my edge. My perspective."

"Yes, that is the way of love, Holmes. And you consider this bad? To love someone so fully, you consider this an evil feeling?"

"No not bad or evil. It is simply that, and I have given this considerable thought over the years, it is simply that when one falls in love, one must soon realize that life is not about just the immediate me anymore. It is the giving and sharing even the smallest of things that makes the love grow and the lover all the more precious. However, when the giving and sharing are gone, one begins to resort to the former selfish ideal once more and the basic narcissistic concept of the brain, such as Freud has written of, takes control and the entire relationship now becomes about the ME. What will I get from this relationship? How will I benefit from this person? What can this person do for me? You see what I am getting at, Watson. Suddenly one forgets why there was the love in the first place and the other party is the one to suffer the damage."

"Are you saying that is what happened between you and Jeannette Dubois?"

"No, Watson, allow me to clarify. Jeannette Dubois loved me heart and soul and I believe would have died for me. As a matter of fact, reading the last few entries, she did just that. She played the same ruse on me as I have done to you on countless occasions, except she was much more clever and brilliant about it. She saved my life far more times than I can ever thank her for.

"No, Watson. Looking back in retrospect, it would have been I in the long term of it that would have destroyed everything. I was the one who could not let go of the past…of who I really was. I was the selfish one, Watson."

"But surely she did not see it that way, Holmes."

"No of course not. Jeannette Dubois was never thinking of herself and she had a way of seeing only the good and overlooking the bad. Her thoughts and actions were always of helping someone else. Look at and read it again. She saved my life. She tried to help her friend Michelle Dutton. She had a heart of gold that is for certain. As I said before, Watson, Jeannette Dubois was simply the kind of woman one MUST fall in love with."

"Yes of course. I never met her or knew her but by your accounts and the words of the diary, I feel as though I've known her all my life."

"That was a period in my life I shall never forget, although I've learned to put it behind me. It was a period of great joy and happiness. I do not regret one moment of my love of Jeannette Dubois and it is finally good to say so aloud!"

It was finally out and I was elated! Sherlock Holmes had finally coming to terms with his past and now I lay my hopes with a full recovery over the diary issue. The whole atmosphere in the room had changed. The sometimes tense moments between us were gone. Once more was the old familiar comfortableness that had existed between Holmes and me.

We replenished our pipes with fresh tobacco and sat in silence each contemplating, thinking, reminiscing in our own minds. It seemed now that it was out in the open, there was a need for silence. I could see through the partially open drapes, the sun begin to rise over the horizon. It looked to be a beautiful day.

"Now, what of the note, Holmes?" I finally broke the silence.

"The note? Yes. It did say our sender should be arriving any time soon. In all my cases and all my years Watson, this one baffles me. There are endless possibilities and it does no good to speculate until all the facts are know."

"And if it surfaces that you have indeed a child out of this?"

"First, I believe I shall not deny it, for I have nothing to be ashamed of. Second, I should tell Mycroft that he is an uncle. And third…

"Third," he leaned towards me with a wide smile that affected his entire face. "Third, Watson, I shall ask you to be my child's godfather."

"Why! Holmes!" I was stunned "But the child is a gown adult by now!'

"And should that matter? Love at any age is always love!" He laughed then, a good hearty, infectious laugh that touched one's very soul. I knew then that he had let go. The contents of the diary were no longer a frightful phantom of the past meant to haunt and torment him. They were meant as a bright blossom of the future. His future.

"Don't get all blubbery on me, old chap. It is a matter of simple deduction. I can think of no one more loving and caring then yourself, Watson, with which to share the love of a child."

We heard the front door open just then and Mrs. Garrett humming as she entered the house. She opened the study door and exclaimed, "Why Mr. Holmes! Dr. Watson! You are certainly up early." She crossed the room and coughed when the thick smoke of the pipe tobacco caught in her throat. "My goodness, one can hardly breathe in here let alone see. It won't do for your visitors, sir." And she drew back the drapes and pushed open the windows. The smoke filtered out as the clean fresh air and sunshine replaced it.

"Visitors?" Holmes asked.

"Why yes, sir. I met them on the lane. A young man and a woman. Said they were looking for Sherlock Holmes and I told them to follow me. They are in the hall, sir. They asked me to give you this."

Mrs. Garrett handed Holmes an envelope and he told her, "Give me one minute, Mrs. Garrett and show them in."

"Very good, sir," and she left.

Holmes opened the envelope and removed an old torn and yellowed newspaper clipping from inside. I did not have to see it to know it was my own article written years ago of the death of Sherlock Holmes. I could see Holmes's eyes light up and linger on the thing, saw him, ever so slightly, bend to sniff the fish smell that must still linger there.

A minute passed and there was a light tap on the door. Mrs. Garrett entered with our guest. "Mr. Holmes, this is Juliet Dutton, come to see you." She gave a short curtsey before leaving, a short but swift glance thrown over her shoulder before closing the study door.

I knew immediately the young woman that entered. She was as Holmes had described. Her black hair hung loose down her shoulders, showing a hint of red in the sunlight that streamed in through the window. Her nose was pert set between two brightly flushed high cheekbones and her lips full and red, showing beautiful white teeth when she smiled. Her eyebrows were arched and perfect one to the other and I knew in an instant how Sherlock Holmes had fallen in love with Jeannette Dubois.

Her eyes rested upon me for an instant and then fell upon my friend. I could see the old familiar hint of excitement in those eyes. Eyes that flashed bright and fiery of a gray-blue and held a look of arresting command. I knew those eyes and knew them well. And as I stared at those eyes I knew…

Those eyes…..

Those eyes were the eyes of Sherlock Holmes.

Made in the USA
Monee, IL
23 November 2021